Alumanaya

A tropical story

about

living with tranquility

Also by Steve Ludwigs

The Alumanaya Travel Guide

Alumanaya - A tropical story
about
living with tranquility
(Audiobook)

Alumanaya Island Art

Available through Palm Canyon Wellness Group, LLC
(314) 482-6152   www.alumanaya.com

Alumanaya

A tropical story
about
living with tranquility

The 5 island principles of
balance and perspective

Steve Ludwigs

Published and distributed in the United States by:
Palm Canyon Wellness Group, LLC
P.O. Box 64, Cottleville, Missouri 63338

Alumanaya – A tropical story about living with tranquility

Library of Congress Catalog Card Number: 2005901959

ISBN Number: 0-9767112-0-6

Printed in the United States of America

This book is dedicated to my wife, Renee.
You are forever the light in my heart.

Contents

Listing of Art (next page)

Island Art

Alumanaya

A tropical story

about

living with tranquility

Introduction

". . . we have more work to do. . . but nobody said we can't have a little fun while we work!"

- Miri

Who doesn't want to live with a tropical island state of mind? Who doesn't dream of warm sunny beaches, the sun reflecting off the gently rolling ocean waves, the palm trees swaying in the breeze? Don't most of us frequently wish we could run away to such a place, leaving the problems and stresses of everyday life behind? But we know we can't really do that. We've got too much going on here and now – the job, family, picking up the cleaning. But what if you could go there in your mind? What if you could take a tropical break whenever you wanted too – even in the middle of your next management meeting or the next disagreement with your kids? How about while sitting in traffic or waiting in a long line for your latte? More seriously, what if you could think of the soothing scent of a warm jasmine breeze or the calming sound of waves tumbling over the sand when you are faced with a real life challenge?

This is a story about the island and people of Alumanaya – a place most of us would call a tropical paradise. But there is more to Alumanaya than great weather and beautiful surroundings. Over generations, the people of the island have developed a way of relating the various parts of their island to life itself. These ideas provide a quick mental escape in a stressful situation – a brief chance to relax and re-charge before jumping back into the fray. They can also help with bigger challenges, suggesting a way of looking at the bigger picture and keeping things in perspective.

This book is not meant to change your life. It's not meant to provide a completely knew way of thinking or transform you into a dreamy sand and surf bum who no longer wears a watch. Unless, of course, that's what you really want! It *is* meant to entertain you and help you to consider that maybe there is a different way of looking at things – a fun way to approach life. If, in the process, you feel a little less stressed (I think you will) and a little more balanced (ditto), then your time on the island has been beneficial.

I originally wrote this book with healthcare professionals in mind – a group of people I greatly admire.

They not only deal with the common everyday issues we all face, but have the added responsibility of caring for others. The story, however, is more universal. The thoughts and ideas can help anyone. If you are a teacher or someone in a "helping" profession, great! This book is for you. If you are in any other profession, including the job of living, this book is for you too.

It's time to begin the journey.

The Journey Begins

"Alumination," Makena said softly as she looked out over the gently rolling ocean waves.

The morning sun had created millions of glistening points of light as the rays bounced off the water. She smiled as she closed her eyes and felt the warm breeze tickle her cheeks and play with her hair. That same breeze was rhythmically coaxing the waves into shore and prompting the palm trees to dance above her.

Makena was in her favorite place on the island. For some, it was Palm Canyon, but for her, it was here on the beach in the shade of this palm grove. This is where she came to think, reflect, appreciate, give thanks, and get direction. This was her refuge, her place to regain and refine her life balance. On an island of beautiful places, this, Makena always thought, was the best.

She was excited for she was about to begin another journey of teaching the ways of her island people. Makena was a Kamua, which, in the language of Alumanaya, meant both teacher and healer. Over the years, Makena had taught many people the principles of the island and how to apply them. Today began another course with another student. This time, however, was special. For this student was Rumbi, her grandson.

As Makena heard Rumbi's laugh, she laughed herself. She opened her eyes to watch as he played one of his favorite games, ocean tag. Rumbi would follow the receding waves down the sand as they hurried back to sea. Then he'd stop and stand straight and tall, bravely daring the water to challenge him. Quickly, another wave would roll in and Rumbi would laugh hysterically as it chased him up the beach. Occasionally, when he wasn't quick enough, the water would catch him, wrapping around his small ankles and washing the sand from beneath his feet. He'd kick and squeal, sending fat drops high in the air. Then, running into the water, he would dive beneath the surface before shooting up to stand waste deep. Rumbi loved the ocean. He loved to play in the warm tropical water. Even at his young age, he somehow knew that the ocean was more than just his playmate and friend; it was a part of him.

"Come, Rumbi," Makena called.

Rumbi ran up the sand to the shady spot under the trees and stood before his grandmother.

"It's time to let the ocean rest for awhile," said Makena as she pulled Rumbi onto her lap. "Besides, we have some things to talk about."

Makena smiled into Rumbi's big brown eyes. She marveled for a moment as she saw in Rumbi, as she had in so many other young people over the years, a profound innocence. The deep, loving, trusting nature instilled in everyone at birth. Makena believed that the essence of life is joy and happiness. Her teachings revolved around that simple concept. We are meant to love and enjoy life. As the elder Kamua on Alumanaya, Makena was not only the primary healer, but also the main teacher of these principles. Keeping these ideas in mind, one could experience "Alumanaya" – a feeling of contentment, perspective and balance, even during difficult times.

"Today, Rumbi," Makena began, "you will begin a great journey."

"Where are we going, Nanua (Rumbi's name for his grandmother)?" Rumbi asked, his eyes growing even bigger.

"This is the greatest journey you will ever make," Makena replied. "But you won't even leave the island. This journey is one that we all take alone, for it is inside of us."

Makena laughed as Rumbi looked down and put his hand on his stomach. "Inside of me?" he questioned, looking back up at her.

"Not in there," Makena said, lightly poking Rumbi in his stomach, "but up here," she said as she softly touched his forehead, "and in here," touching his chest. "This journey is in learning how to live in the ways of our people, learning to experience the true meaning of Alumanaya. The knowing is already there, in your mind and in your heart. The only thing left to do is find and follow the path. But don't worry, I'll help you along the way."

Makena continued, "You see Rumbi, we are all meant to live as happy, loving, joyous people. That's our true nature, although it's often hard, especially if you've forgotten how to do it. Deep down inside, we all know these things, even as little babies. But as we grow older, we forget and need to be reminded. Even you, Rumbi, already know the principles of Alumanaya. Athough you don't think about them much, you experience them every day."

Makena paused as she watched Rumbi try to work through her words. She could tell he was struggling to understand. "Don't worry, Rumbi," she soothed. "You will understand as we go along. Also, it will be fun! Are you ready?"

"Yes!" Rumbi shouted, jumping to his feet, "I'm ready to go! Should I get some coconuts to eat along the way?" He started for the grove of coconut trees down the beach.

"No, no," Makena laughed. "Remember, this journey is inside of you. We're not going anywhere!" Although Makena knew that when one begins this path they will often feel that they have, in fact, traveled to another place.

"Come back and sit down," she said. "Let's get started."

"Sometimes we can't stop life from upsetting even our soul. But remember, the turbulence is only on the surface."

- Makena

Destination One - Ocean

"**O**ur journey begins right now," Makena began, "and lasts the rest of your life. I'm going to tell you how our people have learned to live. These ideas have been passed down over many generations, just as I am passing them along to you. When you are older, you too will pass them along to others. It is the way we are connected to all who have come before and all who are to come. As you hear these principles, some may be a little hard to understand, even though they are quite simple. But harder than understanding them, is keeping them in mind day to day. You see Rumbi, even though these ideas are part of us already, they are easy to forget as we live our lives.

"There are five areas for us to talk about. They are all part of what we experience and have all around us here on Alumanaya. They are the ocean, the wind, the palm trees, the sand, and the sunlight. Each of these surrounds us on our beautiful island. And each of these has something to teach us about how to live our lives. Today, we will begin with the ocean.

"You know how you love to play in the ocean?" Makena asked.

Rumbi nodded.

"Well, there is a reason why that's true, beyond the fact that it's fun and feels good. The ocean, in a very real way, is part of you. You relate to the ocean because it calls to your soul – the very essence of who you are." Makena leaned over and put her hand flat on Rumbi's heart. "Our soul is inside of us, but we can't see it. We can feel it though. Close your eyes and picture in your mind the great ocean before you. See in your mind how big it is. Imagine how deep it is. Think of the beautiful blue color as the sun reflects off the water. Listen to the waves as they tumble up on the sand. Can you see it in you mind?" she asked.

Rumbi nodded again and smiled.

"Good! You've started your journey! How do you feel as you picture the ocean in your mind, imagining how it looks and sounds?"

"Good," said Rumbi, still smiling. "I love the ocean. It feels like home."

"Excellent!" Makena said. "That's right. In a way, it is home, for thinking of the ocean can bring us back to our soul, to where we need to be. You see, Rumbi, the ocean is very, very large. Sometimes it seems endless, stretching out much further than you can see."

Rumbi squinted as he looked out over the waves to the horizon.

"It's also very deep, deeper than we can imagine. In fact, no one has ever been to the deepest parts to explore. We may try to imagine what is there, but we don't really know. Our inner being is much the same. It is vast and endless, deeper than most of us know. Few of us have ever explored the depths of ourselves.

"We all connect with the ocean because what it represents is very similar to our soul – who we are deep down inside. That's why in our journey we relate the ocean to our soul and how it forms the foundation of our way of life. It's also the first step in understanding the feeling of Alumanaya."

Makena paused to let this sink in. She often thought about at what point in life is a person best prepared to begin this journey of understanding. Over the years, she had found that even though all children on Alumanaya begin their education at a young age, she would frequently spend time with older islanders in reminding them of these ideas. She knew that sometimes it's not until someone is quite mature, with many years behind them, before they fully understand and begin to live by the principles. She had seen many people benefit by experiencing a renewed sense of balance and perspective – a sort of tropical tranquility. But not always was everyone receptive. Looking at Rumbi, she couldn't tell if he was ready or not. *Perhaps he is still too young*, she thought. Nevertheless, Makena decided to continue. She would share the principles with her grandson. Whether or not he was ready to hear them was up to him.

"There are many more similarities, Rumbi," Makena continued. "In relating the soul to qualities of the ocean, it makes it easier to understand ourselves. The ocean has always been there and always will be there, the same as our soul. It's deep, powerful, surrounding us everywhere. No matter where you are on the island, even if you can't see it, you know the ocean is always there. You can even hear the ocean when you are in Palm Canyon!"

"How can I hear the ocean from there?" asked Rumbi, thinking of that special part of the island. "I can't even see it from Palm Canyon."

"Remember," said Makena, "the ocean – our soul – is always with us. There is a fun way to remind ourselves of that. Remember how we've played with the shells on beach? Think of how we hold a seashell to our ear and listen for the ocean. Well, we can do that even without the shell. Try this." Makena cupped her hand and held it up to her ear. "Go on, try it."

Rumbi cupped his little hand and held it up to his ear.

Makena laughed as his eyes grew wide.

"It sounds just like the shell!" he cried.

"That's right," Makena said. "See? You don't even need a seashell. Anytime you need to remember that the ocean is always nearby, even when you are in the middle of the island, just hold your hand up to you ear like I showed you. It's a good way to remind yourself of your center, your soul.

"We all need to be constantly reminded of who we are, to remember our essence. For just like the ocean is water, and we need water to survive, so we need our soul to survive. Just like it's impossible for us to live very long without water, the same is true trying to live without feeling our soul. It can't be done."

"Does our soul have waves?" asked Rumbi, looking out to the ocean.

"Yes, in a way it does," said Makena, pleased that Rumbi was thinking about her words.

"That's another way the ocean is similar to our soul. See how the waves look right now?" she asked as she pointed out to the gentle rolling waters. "Watching them, don't they make you feel good, peaceful?"

Rumbi nodded and added, "The waves are friendly today. It's fun being in the water."

"Yes, today is beautiful, but what about when a storm blows in and the waves are tossing and tumbling?" Makena asked.

"They look angry sometimes. I don't want to be in the water then. It's scary," Rumbi replied.

"That's true. It can be dangerous at those times to go into the water. But think of the part of the ocean you actually would get into. Isn't it only the part close to the shore?"

Rumbi thought for a moment, then agreed. "Yes, I only go a little way into the water anyway, even on the friendly days."

"That's right," Makena replied. "Most of us only go a little way into the ocean, even on the good days. On the stormy days, when the waters are rough, we're afraid to go in at all. But think about what the ocean is like a few feet below the surface. What's the water like there?"

Rumbi looked at her and said, "It's wet?"

Makena laughed, "Well, that's true, but think for a minute. Is it as rough a few feet below the surface as it is on top?" Makena hesitated as she realized that Rumbi might not know the answer to her question. He was still young and hadn't been out in the ocean during a storm or even when the waves were much higher than the gentle sea at the moment.

Rumbi surprised her by saying, "I think the water is not as rough below the surface."

"That's right!" Makena exclaimed, amazed at Rumbi's insight. "Just like it sometimes feels in our soul, sometimes things are stormy and turbulent on the surface. But below, the waters are much calmer. Imagine going deeper and deeper into the water. The deeper you go, the more calm and still things are. Even when a stormy punamu is raging on the surface, in the ocean depths everything is peaceful, always the same. Remember, Rumbi, much like the depths of the ocean, your soul is also always constant, always the same. No matter what is going on in your life, even when you feel you are in the middle of your own punamu, your deepest soul is always calm. The trick is trying to remember that in difficult times."

Makena watched Rumbi as he turned to gaze out into the ocean. *He's learning*, she thought. *Maybe he's not too young after all*. She decided that today was a good day for Rumbi to begin his journey. Nevertheless, Makena knew that most people, young or not, can only absorb so much at a time. She knew it was time to bring this first session to a close.

"That's enough for today, Rumbi," Makena said as she stood and put her arm around his shoulders. "You've learned much and had a great start on your journey."

Rumbi turned and leaned into his grandmother's hug.

"Now, go chase those waves. They've been waiting for you to play!" she said.

Rumbi scampered down the beach and into the water. Back home, as he might put it.

Makena smiled again, one of many this day. In a few days she would once again sit down with Rumbi and talk about the next stop along the journey to Alumanaya.

"We have no control over the wind, or life, except in how we react to it."

- Makena

Destination Two – Wind

"**R**UUUMMMBIII," Makena called. "Rumbi, where are you?"

Makena was standing outside her house, which was nestled in the green hills at the base of the old volcano. From here, Makena could see most of the village below. She would frequently sit out in front, in her favorite chair, and watch the people of Alumanaya go about their day. She loved watching the interaction between her neighbors. How they would work together to get the things done that made the village thrive. From here, she could see the open gathering area, close to the center of the village. This was where most of the big events took place. Announcements, elder meetings, weddings, recognition of special accomplishments, and, of course, observing the passing of someone on to the next world, all took place in this important part of the village. From her vantage point, Makena could see many things, but couldn't see what she was looking for at the moment – her grandson.

Suddenly, Makena jumped as she felt a ripple scurry up her back.

"Nanua!" There was a big gecko on you!" Rumbi exclaimed. "I scared him away!"

"Ohhh," Makena said, thinking it felt more like little fingers. "Is that what that was. Thank you for chasing him away. Are you ready to take the next step in your journey?"

"Yes! Let's go," Rumbi said. "I feel like going somewhere fun!"

Makena smiled as she thought how much she enjoyed teaching the ways of her people, especially to someone as eager as Rumbi.

"All right, today we'll talk about another area that is very important – the wind," she said.

"The wind," Rumbi said as he looked up at the gently swaying palm trees. "Are we going to fly?" he asked hopefully.

Makena laughed, "Well, in a way, this whole journey is teaching you to fly. But for today, why don't we just sit right here on the ground."

Rumbi and Makena sat down on a large mat that had been woven from the fibers of a coconut tree. As Makena looked at Rumbi, she could see her reflection in his big brown eyes. *I'm in him, just as he is in me,* she thought.

She was reminded that we are all connected. With this thought, she began.

"The wind and the air, Rumbi, represent life itself. It is all around us, always there. If there was no air, there would be no life." Makena paused to let that thought soak in. "You know how you sometimes take a deep breath and hold it for fun?" she asked.

Rumbi nodded, "I can't hold it very long. My tummy always pushes it out."

"That's right," Makena said. "You can't stop that from happening, just like you can't stop life from happening. The trick is learning how to flow with your life. Taking in only what you need to serve you the best and letting the rest go on by."

Makena could see this last part may have gone a little over Rumbi's head. His puzzled look showed he was trying hard to understand, but Makena knew things weren't very clear to him. *That's fine*, she thought, *most people don't understand this concept in the beginning. It usually takes a little practice for things to make more sense.*

"Try this," Makena said. "Close your eyes and feel the breeze on your face." Makena smiled as she watched Rumbi do as she asked. "How does it feel?"

"Good. It feels like a monkey tickling my nose!" Rumbi giggled as he half-opened one eye.

"A monkey!" Makena exclaimed. "I'll show you how a monkey tickles!" She reached over and wrapped Rumbi up in her arms while tickling his sides with her fingers.

"Stop it, Nanua!" Rumbi cried as he laughed and tried to tickle her too.

Makena and Rumbi tumbled over on the mat, laughing even harder.

"OK, OK," Makena said as she took a breath and wiped her eyes. "Enough of this goofing around. This is a serious journey." She sat back up and gave Rumbi her best back-to-business look. Rumbi wasn't fooled. He saw the slight smile on her lips and the twinkle in her eyes. He was having fun and knew she was too. Makena appreciated Rumbi's ability to enjoy the process of his journey. She was happy that she didn't have to remind him to have fun along the way.

"As I was saying," Makena began again, "the air, like life, is always around us. As you take each breath, you are living life. The events of life will continue to come along even if you try to stop them. Much like trying to hold your breath, you can't do it for very long before . . . here it comes again. Sometimes life will seem harder than at other times. For example, remember how last week the wind blew very hard and the trees were bending and rattling against each other?"

Rumbi nodded.

"Well, that's how life feels sometimes, difficult and a little out of control. It may feel a little scary, but just as we can't stop the wind, we also can't stop life. We can't just hold our breath to keep things from happening. We can't control the wind, but we can decide how we react to it." Makena paused as Rumbi looked at her intently. Somehow she knew that he understood her.

"What we want to learn is to take only what we need from life and let the rest go. Just as we take the breath we need from each breeze and allow the rest of the air to flow on past us. When the wind is blowing hard, meaning you are having a difficult time in life, sometimes all you can do is continue to breathe, taking only what you need and letting the rest go. Remember, the wind will always eventually die down and life will be calm again.

"All right, Rumbi, close your eyes again and feel the breeze on your face," Makena said. "How does the air feel now?"

"Warm . . . full," Rumbi said.

"Now," Makena said, "take a deep breath and think of how you are just drawing in a fraction of the air around you. Imagine the rest of the breeze flowing on past, carrying what you don't need, your troubles, with it."

Rumbi took a deep breath and let it out slowly. He smiled. Even with his eyes closed, the content look on his face told Makena he had reached the second milestone in his journey.

"That's all for today," Makena said as she once again leaned over and wrapped her arms around Rumbi. This time she hugged him close and said, "You are a good traveler, Rumbi. I'm so happy to be on this journey with you. Now, run off and find one of those monkeys that were around earlier!"

Rumbi jumped up and looked at Makena. "I'll look for the monkeys, Nanua," he said, "but you better watch out for those geckos!"

He turned and ran down the path. Makena could hear him laughing long after he was out of sight.

"Like grains of sand, our many thoughts and emotions are also shifting. Learn to arrange you own internal beach in a beautiful way."

- Makena

Destination Three – Sand

As Makena walked along the beach, she could feel the warmth of the sand flowing up through her toes. Thinking about the sand and how it, like the rest of the island, was part of the life of her people, Makena remembered the many times she had tried to explain it's meaning – how it fit into the bigger picture of Alumanayan life. *It's not always easy for people to understand*, she thought. *How am I going to explain it to a young boy?*

She stopped to gaze at the clouds far out on the horizon and silently asked for guidance on how to talk to Rumbi in a way he would comprehend. Watching the puffy white forms slowly change shape, she thought of how the same thing happens to the sand on the beach. She looked back at where she had walked. The waves had already washed away her footprints. *Things are always changing*, she thought. *That's the main thing to understand.* She thought of how much Rumbi loved the beach. He had played in the sand since he was barely able to crawl. She hoped he would understand her next message.

Smiling a thank you for the inspiration, she set out to find her grandson.

It didn't take long. A few steps further down the beach, Makena heard familiar laughter drifting though the palm trees.

"Ruummbiii," she called. "Rumbi, is that you?"

"Nanua," she heard him answer from off towards the hills. "Here I come."

Rumbi bolted from a palm grove, ran down the beach and collapsed at her feet. "I was being chased by a wild pig!" he said, his eyes wide with excitement and mischief.

"A wild pig!" Makena exclaimed, "Why, I haven't seen any wild pigs around here in a long time."

"He was THIS big," said Rumbi, spreading his arms as wide as he could. "He had stinky hair and big teeth. I think he wanted to eat me!"

Rumbi broke into wild laughter as he pretended to hide behind Makena's skirt. "Save me, Nanua! Save me!"

"A wild, little-boy-eating pig! We'd better run!" said Makena as she grabbed Rumbi's hand and started down the beach.

Rumbi knew that he hadn't fooled his Nanua. "Well, he's probably gone now. I think we're safe," he said.

"I hope so. But if he comes back, I'm glad you're here to protect me," Makena said. She could see Rumbi stand taller with the idea that his Nanua thought he was big enough to take care of her.

"I'll watch out for him," he said, happy to play along.

"In the meantime," Makena said, "let's talk about the next step on your journey."

"OK," said Rumbi. "Where are we going this time?"

"We're already here," said Makena as she sat down on the beach. "Today, we're going to talk about how our feelings, and the thoughts we have, are always changing. A way for us to understand that is to think of the sand."

"The sand?" said Rumbi, picking up a powdery-white handful.

"Think of the sand on the beach as like the thoughts that are in here," Makena reached over and touched Rumbi on his forehead. "Every day, you have many, many thoughts swimming around in your head, just like the many grains of sand on the beach. Many things can affect those thoughts, and so, how you feel. We've already talked about some of them, like the ocean and the wind. Do you remember talking about how the ocean is like your soul?"

Rumbi nodded slowly. Makena could tell he was thinking hard about what that had to do with the sand on the beach.

"And," she continued, "remember when we talked about the wind and how we relate that to life?"

Again, Rumbi nodded, still a little lost.

"Well, both the ocean and the wind affect the sand, don't they? The ocean washes up the beach and rearranges the sand, doesn't it? And the wind, when it's strong, can blow the sand a long way, can't it?"

"Yes," said Rumbi. "Sometimes, when the waves are angry and wild, they wash away whole parts of the beach."

"Right," said Makena. "A way to think of that is; when our soul is in turmoil – like the stormy ocean – our thoughts and emotions are upset also, just like the way the turbulent water can move the sand around on the beach."

Makena paused to let Rumbi think about that.

"But when the waves are gentle, they make pretty shapes in the sand," Rumbi said.

"Yes, they do." Makena said. "That's what happens when the soul is calm and centered. Our thoughts are positive and hopeful, which makes us feel good. Just like the calm ocean water washes the sand clean."

Makena marveled at Rumbi's understanding. Sometimes it was actually much easier to teach a young child. They hadn't yet been affected by too many tough life experiences. Sometimes their simple way of thinking was the best way to learn.

"But when the wind blows hard, sand is sometimes blown all the way into our village, isn't it?" Makena continued. "That doesn't make us very happy when we have to sweep it out of our houses, does it?"

Rumbi shook his head, "No, I don't like it when we have to sweep. I'd rather play with Polo."

"I know you would," said Makena, thinking about how much Rumbi loved his pet parrot. "But remember what we learned about the wind? Sometimes it's going to blow more than we would like and that may not make us very happy. But we need to remember that it's just the way life is. We're not able to stop the wind from blowing, or life from happening, but we *can* choose how we feel about it. We can re-arrange our thoughts like we can sweep the sand out of our house."

Makena paused to allow Rumbi to absorb this last analogy. She knew that this was one of the most important parts of today's lesson – knowing that we can't control the wind, or life – but we can react in a positive way to help ourselves feel good. Just like we can clean up the scattered sand.

"And," she began again, "remember also how the wind can affect the ocean, causing rough, stormy waters. We can't always keep that from happening. Sometimes we can't stop life from upsetting even our soul. But remember, the turbulence is only on the surface. As we go a little deeper, it's calm again. Our goal is to try and keep the surface calm too, so, as you've pointed out, the gentle waves make pretty shapes in the sand rather than washing away the beach."

"Don't worry, Nanua," Rumbi said. "The beach will always be here. It'll never completely wash away."

Makena smiled as she thought how Rumbi's affirmation was much more powerful than he realized. Her hope was that he would always remember it.

"All right, that's enough for today," said Makena. "How are you enjoying your journey?"

"It's fun!" said Rumbi. "I like going to new places without ever leaving home. Where are we going next?"

"We have two more stops," answered Makena. "But those are for another day. It's time for us to go back to the village. You'd better walk with me, just in case you have to protect me from that wild pig!"

Makena and Rumbi headed down the beach towards the village. The sand felt soft and warm around their feet.

"You are like a tall palm tree with deep roots. Strong, but flexible, you can bend with the stormy winds and then stand up straight again."

- Makena

Destination Four – Palm Tree

Makena walked through the village looking for her grandson.

"Have you seen Rumbi?" she asked Peule, the village artist.

"Not recently," he replied. "But I did see him running towards the trail to Palm Canyon earlier this morning."

"Palm Canyon!" said Makena as she looked up the hill to where the path leading to the sacred island spot began. "Surely he wouldn't try to walk all that way by himself!"

Thinking how she hadn't found him anywhere else, Makena decided that probably was exactly what Rumbi had decided to do.

As Makena made her way up the hill, she said a quick prayer for her grandson's safety. It wasn't that there were any real dangers on the trail, on in Palm Canyon itself, but to a little boy, many things could be scary. If Rumbi had decided to explore, she hoped he was alright.

Starting down the trail, Makena thought about the many times she had made this journey. For the people of

Alumanaya, Palm Canyon was the most sacred place on the island. There, and only there, grew the Alumanaya Palm tree. The islanders thought this particular palm had the power to heal both the mind and the body. They often visited Palm Canyon to look at and touch the special trees. Some even gathered a few fronds to bring back to the village. Interestingly, every time someone would bring back a portion of a palm, it would soon turn brown and dry. Many attempts at transplanting an Alumanaya Palm had all ended in failure, with the tree slowly dying. Nevertheless, the villagers still brought back the leaves to decorate their houses. Some would draw pictures and make sculptures of the palms to help them remember their visits to Palm Canyon.

Makena had always thought that the reason the Alumanaya Palm would only grow in Palm Canyon was precisely to draw the people back to the sacred area. The islanders needed to be constantly reminded of the principles of life and regularly making the journey to Palm Canyon helped greatly in that. Spending quiet time appreciating the trees, the waterfall, and the clean, gentle breezes was what helped them remember what was important. There was a sense of life and healing in Palm Canyon. But Makena knew that it wasn't really the Alumanaya Palm tree that caused this. Rather, it was the islander's belief that was the real power. As part of her teaching, she tried to help them to understand that the belief was with them at all times and that even when they couldn't be there physically, they could always go to Palm Canyon – and feel Alumanaya – in their minds.

Makena had been walking for a while when she thought she heard something. She stopped to listen. Yes, there it was again. It sounded like a small voice singing. "Rumbi, is that you?" Makena called.

"Nanua!" Rumbi cried out. "You're here!"

From around a bend in the trail, Rumbi ran full speed into Makena's arms.

"Nanua!" Rumbi said, pulling in close to his grandmother.

"Are you alright?" Makena asked, feeling him tremble.

"I was scared," Rumbi said. "I wanted to go to Palm Canyon, but I didn't think it would be so far. I got really, really tired and decided to sit and rest for a while."

"But I thought I heard someone singing. Was that you?" Makena asked.

"Yes," said Rumbi. "I remembered how one time you told me that singing always makes you feel good. So I thought I'd sing to make myself feel better and give me more energy. I was singing some of the songs we sing at the gathering place."

"Did it help?" asked Makena as she stroked Rumbi's hair. She could tell he had been scared but was quickly feeling better now that she was there.

"Yes," Rumbi replied. "When I wasn't singing, I was thinking of the music in my head. It helped remind me of the fun times we've had."

Makena smiled to think of Rumbi, alone and scared, singing to chase away his apprehensions. She also thought of how easily Rumbi could admit his fear. As he gets older, she knew that would be harder for him to do.

"Singing was a good idea," Makena said. "That can always help you to feel better! Do you want to go on to Palm Canyon?"

"Yes! Let's go!" Rumbi said, his enthusiasm for adventure returning. "I want to see the waterfall!"

Rumbi had already been to Palm Canyon a few times. The first time had been shortly after he was born. Makena had carried him there in his small baby pouch. It was common for the islanders to take infants to Palm Canyon to experience the beauty and sense of peace early in life. The children don't remember the first few visits, but somewhere deep inside, the feeling usually takes hold and can be recalled whenever they think of Palm Canyon. Later, as they get older, they start to pick out their favorite things about the area. The waterfall is especially popular. It had always been Rumbi's favorite part to visit.

They walked on the trail for a while longer until, rounding a bend, they were treated to a breathtaking sight. Spread before them was Palm Canyon. From their spot on the hill they could see the slopes of the red rock walls framing each side, the lush green growth – dotted with colorful flowers – covering the canyon floor, the many Alumanaya Palms, and, far off in the distance, the waterfall.

"We're here!" cried Rumbi as he began running down the trail. "Hurry, Nanua, let's go to the waterfall."

Makena hurried after her grandson, sharing his excitement. She always felt good when she arrived at this spot. The initial view from the hill was one of the mental pictures she often thought of when she wanted to remember the calm tranquility of Palm Canyon. She felt that as often as she had been here physically, she had been here in her mind much more often. *Deep inside, I never really leave*, she thought.

She caught up with Rumbi just as he jumped into the pool at the base of the waterfall. Along with her grandson,

Makena liked the waterfall too. She liked to sit on the smooth rocks at the waters edge and look into the cool, emerald depths. She liked listening to the sparkling fresh stream gurgle and sing as it tumbled down over the red rocks. She often imagined she could see the true spirit of the island reflecting in the colorful rainbows that flashed in the drifting spray.

As she watched Rumbi splash, Makena thought about how the water is continually on its own journey. From its source high in the green hills, it flows through Palm Canyon and on to the village, finally spilling into the ocean. The clouds then pull the moisture out of the waves and drop the rain back on the mountain. The idea of the endless flow always seemed to calm her and establish a sense of permanence in her world.

Rumbi climbed, dripping, out of the water to sit on the large rock with Makena.

"Rumbi, remember the journey we've been on the past few weeks?" Makena asked.

"You mean to get to Palm Canyon? That didn't take weeks Nanua, that's just today," Rumbi said.

Makena laughed, "No, not the short trip we just made to get here. I mean the bigger journey we're making in learning about how to live our lives."

"Oh," said Rumbi. "You mean with the ocean and wind and sand!"

"That's the one. Well, we have another part of that to talk about. And this is a great place to do it," she said as she looked towards a grove of Alumanaya Palms.

"So far, we've been talking about how we think about things in here," Makena said as she tapped Rumbi gently on his forehead. "And how we feel things in here," she said as she touched him on his chest, near his heart. "Today, we're going to talk about the rest of the inside and outside of you." Makena tickled her fingers quickly all over Rumbi as he giggled.

"Stand up, close your eyes, and imagine your whole body as a palm tree," Makena said. "Pretend your arms are like the palm fronds, gently swaying in the breeze. Your middle is like the trunk, strong and straight, and your legs are like the roots, firmly planted in the ground. Can you see that in your mind?" she asked.

Rumbi nodded, his eyes closed. "Is my head a coconut?" he asked.

Makena laughed, "Well, sometimes your head can be as *hard* as a coconut! If you want to make that part of your mental picture, that's fine. Whatever helps you to better see yourself.

"Now, think of how the tall palm trees sway with the ocean winds. Bend over forward a little, then to the left side, then to the right side. Imagine the warm breeze is moving you around."

Makena smiled as Rumbi did as she asked. "Good! Now, slowly move your arms up and down and all around. Let your hands and fingers dance with the same gentle ocean breeze." Makena marveled at how gracefully Rumbi moved. She was always amazed at how people could look so content while doing this. And how they always seemed to have a smile on their face.

"OK, now open your eyes. How did that feel?" Makena asked.

"That was fun!" said Rumbi. "I was the tallest palm tree on the island!"

"Yes, you looked pretty tall to me," said Makena. "With a very big coconut for a head! Now, look around. How many different types of palm trees do you see?"

Slowly turning in a circle, Rumbi said, "I see a lot. And there are many different sizes and shapes."

"That's right," Makena said. "But no matter what each looks like, if it's tall or short, big or small, all are made to live in a strong and healthy way. As each palm tree grows, it develops strong roots in order to keep it firmly grounded. And, as it gets taller, the trunk is tough, but flexible. Remember how you just now pretended to be a tree moving with the breeze?"

Rumbi nodded.

"That's the same thing a palm tree does. It sways gently in the calm ahani breeze, but it's also made to withstand even scary punamu winds. While it's very strong at the base, it is able to bend in a storm."

"The tallest trees bend the most," Rumbi said.

"Yes, they do," Makena said. "As they grow, they may experience many difficulties, but as long as they receive the things they need to remain strong, like regular sunlight and water, they will continue to grow into the beautiful things we appreciate so much.

"So, in difficult times, if you think of yourself as a strong palm tree, with deep, strong roots, you can withstand the high storm winds and eventually stand up straight again. Remember, the winds will always blow, but the palm tree is able to be flexible and bend with the wind. That's the way they survive on the island."

"Do I need sunlight and water too?" Rumbi asked.

"Yes," Makena said. "And you need the good food we have on our island. But you also need to regularly think about and practice the ideas we've been talking about on our journey. It all works together, each part depending on the other. Just like the palm tree needs it's nourishment from water and light to thrive.

"All right, that's enough for today. Speaking of our island food, I'm hungry. Are you ready to go back to the village and get something to eat?"

"OK," said Rumbi. "But can we come back to Palm Canyon soon? I didn't get to play in the waterfall very long."

"Yes, we'll come back," said Makena. "But in the meantime, remember, you can always visit Palm Canyon in your mind whenever you want to."

Makena took Rumbi's hand as they began their journey back to the village. *One more thing to talk about on our bigger journey*, Makena thought. *In a few days, it will be time for the last stop.*

"Come on, Nanua, let's run!" Rumbi said as he scampered up the trail.

"Imagine you can feel the light soaking into your body, through your skin, filling you with strength and courage."

- Makena

Destination Five – Light

Makena sat in front of her house on the hill. The early morning sun had just appeared above the distant ocean horizon and was still low behind the palm trees. She watched as the increasing strength of the light lit the palm fronds from behind, causing them to glow with life. The sparkling of the dew on the flowers lit up her yard with sharp pinpoints of glittering color.

Today, I'll talk with Rumbi about the final destination on our journey, she decided. To Makena, this final principle of the Alumanayan people always seemed to pull things together. She always thought it was actually more like a part of each of the other four than something separate. She also knew that it could be both the easiest and most difficult to understand and apply. She was proud of how Rumbi, in his small-child way, had been able to easily think about and accept the things they had talked about so far. In many ways, Rumbi had already moved further down the path to Alumanaya than many of the older islanders. Makena knew, however, that everyone had his or her own understanding and that it would come at the proper time. Sometimes sooner, sometimes later. Makena also knew that it was not just learning about each point, but the ability to apply the principles in everyday life that was important. Usually, that was the biggest challenge. She hoped that Rumbi would be able to remember the things he had learned as the winds of his life would blow.

Many mornings, Rumbi would come to his grandmother's house to share her breakfast of fresh mangoes, papaya, and bananas. Today, Makena had also baked sweetnut bread. This was always one of Rumbi's favorites. The warm, rich smell was just beginning to permeate the morning air, mingling with the sweet scent of the flowers. As surely as if she had called him, the aroma soon had Rumbi bouncing up the trail to her house.

"Is that bread I smell?" Rumbi said when he saw Makena.

"It sure is! I thought that would bring you to my house this morning. It's almost ready. Come and help me with it."

Rumbi followed Makena over to the oven that was cut into the side of the hill.

"Be patient. It needs to cool a little," Makena said as she pulled the bread from the hot lava rocks. She smiled as she saw how excited Rumbi was to get a taste. She loved how the smallest things could delight him.

Makena cut fruit into bowls for each of them, then broke off a big piece of the warm bread and handed it to Rumbi.

"Let's go sit down. We have something to talk about," Makena said.

"Ummmm," Rumbi answered, his mouth full.

They sat at the small table under a Banyan tree.

"Rumbi," Makena began, "we've been talking the last few weeks about our journey and today it's time for the last step."

"Will we get a prize for completing the trip?" Rumbi asked.

"Well, in a way, yes we will," Makena replied. "But not the sort of prize you may be thinking. The reward won't be anything you can really see or hold, it will be something you can feel. And, if you use this prize, it will be more valuable than anything you could ever have. Also, we never really finish this journey. It's something we all do our whole lives. Our real goal is not so much to get to the destination, but to be happy, joyful and at peace along the way.

"So far, we've talked about the ocean, the wind, the sand and the palm trees. Today, we're going to talk about something that is part of all of them – light."

"Light," said Rumbi, thoughtfully. "You mean, like from the sun?"

"Yes, the sunlight is a big part of what I mean. But from where else do we get light?" Makena asked.

"Well, light comes from the moon and stars too," Rumbi said, thinking hard. "And I heard someone say one time that there are fish in the ocean that glow!"

"Yes, there are!" Makena said. "And light comes from many other things. How about the fires we make at the gathering place? Or the glow of the lava rocks that baked the bread? We can sometimes see light from the top of the volcano and also from the fireflies at night. You see, Rumbi, there is light everywhere. But the light I'm speaking of is not just what we can see, it's what we can feel inside."

"There's a light inside of me?" Rumbi said, looking down at his stomach.

"Yes, there is," said Makena. "Do you know how I know? I can see it in the sparkle in your eyes and in the moisture that glistens on your skin when you run. I can also see it in your smile, hear it in your laugh, feel it in your touch when you hug me. You are full of light Rumbi!"

"So, when it's dark outside, I can just shine my own

light so I won't trip over the rocks and roots on the trail," said Rumbi excitedly.

Makena smiled. Once again, Rumbi had unknowingly found the key to her talk. "Yes, you can. But it may not be exactly as you think! It's not like pointing your finger to illuminate the path in front of you. It's more like always knowing that the light is there, inside of you and everywhere around you. And it will guide you on your journey."

Makena paused as she let her words wash over Rumbi. She knew this was a hard concept to grasp and wasn't sure Rumbi would understand.

"But what about when the sun drops into the ocean? There's no more light then," Rumbi said.

"It may seem like that," Makena said, "but the sun isn't really gone, it's always in the same place. We're the ones who have moved! Soon, our island comes back around to where we can see the sun again. Just like we saw it come up this morning.

"Think of how, on some days, it's cloudy and the light doesn't seem as bright. Actually, the light is as bright as ever, it's just covered by a few clouds. And even at night, what about the light from the moon and stars? The light is always there, Rumbi, in many ways and many forms. It will never leave you. No matter what.

"Let's walk for a little bit and look for light in other things," Makena said, wanting Rumbi to understand a little better.

"See how the sunlight shines on the flowers?" Makena pointed out. "Doesn't it make them bright and colorful?"

Rumbi nodded.

A gecko scurried across the path in front of them. "Look how the sunlight bounces off his back? See how bright and green he looks?"

Rumbi nodded again and smiled, "And the light makes Polo shine – bright blue and green and yellow and red." He was starting to understand.

As they walked through the village, they saw many other things brought to life by the light. They saw the flash of the knife as the artist carved the wood and the sparkle of the water in the stream that ran though the center of the village. Standing on the bridge, Rumbi pointed out the shimmering scales of the fish as they drifted lazily in the water.

The passing villagers smiled at Makena and her grandson.

"Can you see the light in their faces?" Makena asked Rumbi.

"Yes. They're happy and that makes me feel good!" he replied.

Once more, Makena was struck by how Rumbi could easily arrive at the heart of her lessons. One of the things she wanted to impress upon him was how someone could feel the light inside themselves and then transfer that sense of joy and happiness into another. That was one of the ways the healers on the island would help people to feel better.

Makena and Rumbi arrived at the beach and paused to look out over the ocean.

"Look how the light flashes off the waves," Makena said.

"It makes them look warm and fun!" Rumbi exclaimed. "I want to go play with them!"

"You can soon, but let's look around a little more first," Makena said. "What other ways do you see light?"

They began to walk on the beach and Rumbi said, "Look, the light makes the grains of sand flicker like little stars."

"Yes, it does. What else do you see?" said Makena.

Rumbi ran a few steps to pick up a seashell. "Look at how the light shines on the inside of the shell. It looks white, but I can see many other colors in there too!"

"I see the colors. What a pretty shell," said Makena. "Anything else?"

Rumbi slowly turned in a circle. "Everywhere. Light is everywhere. I can feel it inside me too, like you said. It feels warm."

"Good! Makena said. "I'm happy you see that light is indeed everywhere, including inside you. Let's do one more thing. Stand up straight, like a tall palm tree, and close your eyes. Now, slowly breath in and imagine your are breathing in the light that is all around you."

Makena watched as Rumbi did as she asked.

"Imagine that you can feel the light soaking into your body, through your skin, filling you up."

Rumbi breathed deeply and smiled. "It feels good. It's lighting me up inside!"

"Yes, it is," said Makena. "It's filling you with strength, joy and happiness. Try it again."

Rumbi took another deep breath. "Whenever I come to the beach, I'm going to do this," he declared. "I like it!"

"That's a great idea," Makena said. "But you don't have to wait to get to the beach to do it. You can do this anywhere and at anytime. Remember, the light is everywhere, even when it is dark. You can always soak in the light whenever you want. It will give you strength and help you to feel better.

"All right, that's enough talk for today. What do you want to do now?" Makena asked, already knowing what he wanted.

"I'll show you!" Rumbi yelled as he ran down the beach into the waves. He kicked at the water throwing spray high into the air. "Look Nanua, I'm making stars!"

The sunlight glittering on the water drops did indeed look like stars, Makena thought. She marveled at how the light can bring such power, even to a little boy.

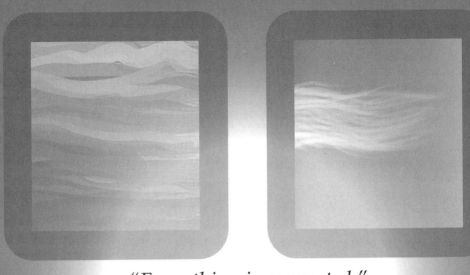

"Everything is connected."

- Makena

Summary

Makena again was in her favorite spot on the island. From the shade of the palm grove she gazed out over the ocean. But her attention was not on the waves or the lazy clouds drifting in the sky. She was thinking of Rumbi and the journey of teaching they had recently completed. Makena hoped she had been able to say things in such a way that Rumbi, even if he didn't fully understand, would at least consider the principles of his fellow islanders. Makena knew that everyone heard their own truth in their own time. Was this the right time for her grandson? She was comforted in the knowing that the words and approach she had taken with Rumbi didn't really come from her, but came from somewhere far beyond, from the depths of her ancestors and, from the light itself. She also knew that however Rumbi chose to use the principles, it was up him.

Makena thought back to the many people she had spoken with over the years, teaching the ways of her people. She knew that the ideas are very simple but could have a dramatic impact on those who really think about them. She knew there must be other islands and different ways to think about how to live life. Makena knew that was alright too. In the end, all paths lead to the same place.

Makena thought about how, in relating the parts of their island world to life, the people of Alumanaya have, over many years, discovered a way of living that they found could help them through difficult times. In remembering the vast, powerful ocean, they understand their inner strength. Thinking of the constant island winds reminds them that life is always happening. They can't stop it, but they can take just what they need from it and move on. Realizing that their thoughts and emotions are constantly shifting like the sand on the beach reminds them that while life can present challenges, they have the power to arrange their thinking to best serve them and keep them in peace. In relating their body to the palm tree, they remember to be flexible, but have strong roots to withstand the storms. Finally, understanding that the light is always there, everywhere, gives them hope in the darkest times as well as bringing joyous life to the bright days.

While Makena hoped for Rumbi joy, peace, and tranquility in his life, she knew that he would have struggles, as all people do. Rumbi would certainly face difficult challenges and would need the strength and comfort from the ideas she had tried to provide. In time, Rumbi would learn to use the principles of his people.

Makena said a quick thank you prayer for the help that had been provided in her teaching and rose to make her way back to the village. She smiled when thinking of Rumbi and his small-child innocence and joy. She paused to breathe in the clean ocean air and feel the warm sun on her skin. From somewhere down the beach, she could hear the faint sound of a young boy's laughter as he played in the gentle ocean waves.

Rumbi's Adventure

R umbi awoke to the sound of a restless parrot.
      Polo must be ready for breakfast, he thought.
I'll feed him as soon as I get up.

Rumbi rolled over to look out the window of his small room in the house he shared with his aunt, Anate. He could see the tops of the palm trees waving at him, calling him to come out and play. To Rumbi, practically everything on the island was a playmate. The palm trees, the ocean, the deep red lava rocks – all were there for him to explore and enjoy.

"Sqaauuuk," said Polo again.

"OK, OK, I'm coming," said Rumbi as he climbed out of his hammock. He grabbed a handful of the crushed macadamia nuts that were sitting in a bowl next to Polo's perch.

"Here you go," he offered the bird. Rumbi always wondered why Polo didn't just get the nuts for himself. After all, he wasn't in a cage and the nuts were sitting in an open bowl practically right next to him. But Rumbi liked talking to Polo and always laughed when Polo "talked" back to him, so he didn't mind handing him his food.

Thank you, thought Polo. He liked it much better when he could eat his food out of Rumbi's hand. He knew he could get to the nuts anytime he wanted and often did just that, but he much preferred the contact with his human friend.

"You silly bird," said Rumbi, not knowing what Polo was thinking or that the parrot could think at all. "I've got to go. I'll see you later."

Rumbi bounded out through his house and into the front yard where his aunt was enjoying her breakfast.

"Well, there you are sleepyhead. I thought you were going to sleep all day," she said as she hugged him good morning. "I've got some good things for you." She reached for a bowl that was filled with island fruit.

"I'm too busy to eat," said Rumbi. "I've got important things to do."

"Well, in order to do them right, you have to eat properly first," she said with a mock stern look. "I'll put your breakfast in a little bag for you to take with you. Make sure you eat everything."

She handed Rumbi the food in a netted pouch made from the fibers of a coconut tree. Rumbi tied the pouch around his waist, allowed his aunt to kiss him on the forehead, and headed off down the trail towards the center of the village.

"Stay in the village or close by on the beach," she called as she watched him disappear.

"I will. I'll be back for lunch," Rumbi answered back through the trees.

As Rumbi ran, he was sorting through the many things he could do. Today somehow felt like a big day, but he didn't know why. *I could play in the ocean,* he thought. But that didn't seem too interesting, he did that practically every day. *I could watch Peule paint,* he thought. He always enjoyed that. He loved to watch as the bright colors came to life to reveal some new part of the island. He also liked listening to the artist tell his stories about life on the island. Peule had told him many tales about how the island of Alumanaya came to be, what life was like many years ago, the different people he had known. Rumbi always laughed when he talked about how the various animals on the island and in the sea could, in their own way, think and talk too. Rumbi would think of Polo.

"He can't think, he's just a bird," Rumbi always said, laughing.

"You might be surprised," Peule would reply with a wink.

What Rumbi liked the most was when the artist talked about his travels. He told Rumbi about paddling his canoe to other islands where other people lived. These trips always seemed filled with adventure and excitement. Rumbi always wondered why Peule would ever come back to Alumanaya, with so many exciting things to see in other places. *Those islands must be more fun that here*, Rumbi always thought. *Someday, I'm going to see them myself.* Rumbi decided he would stop by the artist's house on the edge of the village to see what he was doing.

As Rumbi entered the village gathering place, he went directly to the stream which flowed down from the hills all the way from Palm Canyon. He liked to stand on the small bridge and watch the brightly colored fish as they slowly circled around, hoping for a few crumbs dropped in the water. This was the center of village activity – where the people would come to celebrate the many events of island life. Whenever someone got married, a new baby was born or one of the fishermen came home with a particularly big fish, everyone gathered here to share in the delight. At certain times of the year, festivals to celebrate past important events were held. Rumbi loved those. They usually meant lots of food, music, dancing and games. The people of Alumanaya loved to celebrate and there never seemed to be a shortage of reasons to be thankful. Even when one of their fellow villagers passed on, the gathering was joyful, remembering and appreciating the best parts of the life just completed.

As Rumbi watched the people of the village carrying out their morning duties, he thought he heard the faint sound of music carried on the breeze. He looked out towards the ocean where he knew Melehono lived. Melehono created the music of the island. He was always part of every event and celebration. Rumbi loved to watch him play the many instruments he had made from things on the island, amazed at how he could make the sounds he could. The older villagers appreciated the feeling Melehono put in his songs. Rumbi heard them talk about how meaningful the words were and had even seen tears in the eyes of some people when he would sing a slow song about island life. Rumbi didn't listen much to the words, he liked the lively music better. He would always jump and hop around like a gecko skittering across the hot sand.

Yes, there it was again. Melehono was playing something. *Probably working on a new tune to play at the next celebration*, Rumbi thought.

Rumbi couldn't decide what to do. He had planned on going to visit Peule and ask him to tell about one of his traveling adventures, but now he was more interested in what Melehono was creating. A few more notes trickled through the trees and Rumbi's mind was made up. This time, the music won out and Rumbi headed off towards the beach and the musician's house.

Although he didn't know exactly where it was, Rumbi had heard that Melehono lived down the trail leading to Lookout Rock. He hoped he could find the way. He decided to let his ears lead him and just follow the music.

As he neared the house, Rumbi slowed down. He had never actually talked to Melehono before or even been near him. The musician was very popular with the people and was considered to be a very important person on the island. *What if he doesn't want me around? I'm probably just bothering him,* he thought.

He stopped on the trail and tried to decide what to do. *Maybe I'll go visit him some other time*, he decided and started to turn back towards the village. But then he again heard the music, a little louder this time. There was something about the tune. It seemed to be calling to him, beckoning him to come join in. Overcoming his hesitation, Rumbi slowly resumed walking. Soon he came to a clearing in the trees and saw a small house on the edge of where the palm grove met the beach.

This must be it, Rumbi thought, as he crouched down behind a Yellowberry bush. He crawled a little further and poked his head around the flowers. He could see the musician sitting in front of his house under a tall palm tree. He was looking out at the ocean and slowly picking the strings on his kikani. The instrument had been carved from the trunk of a mahogany tree and fitted with 8 strings of tightly braided coconut fibers. Rumbi loved the sound it made and always liked watching Melehono play it at the celebrations.

Today, Melehono seemed to be working on a new song. He kept playing the same part over and over, trying things a little differently each time. Rumbi decided he'd stay behind the bushes for a while to watch and listen.

"The waves they are calling, come follow and roam," Melehono sang. He picked a few strings, paused, then began again, *"But now the sunlight reflecting, shows the path to our home."* He picked a few more notes. *"Far we have traveled, many things we have done. Now we're returning to our island . . . to our island . . . "*

"OF FUN!" Rumbi heard himself shout.

Rumbi's eyes flew open wide, realizing what had happened. He ducked down in the bushes, trying to make himself invisible.

"Well, what was that?" said Melehono, looking around. "I think I just heard a singing monkey. I'd better go have a look, maybe he can help me finish this song." He leaned his kikani against the tree, got up and headed towards Rumbi's hiding place.

"Now, where could that monkey be?" Melehono stood with his hands on his hips in front of the bush where Rumbi was hiding. "He may be waaay up in the tree," he said, looking up. "Or, maybe he's looking for fallen coconuts . . . IN THIS BUSH!" He reached in and grabbed Rumbi, pulling him up and out. "Here he is, the singing monkey!"

He plopped Rumbi down on his feet and took a step back. "Well, young monkey, where did you come from?" he asked.

Rumbi looked down at the sand. He had never been this close to the musician before. He was afraid Melehono might be upset with him for interrupting his song.

"I . . . I came from . . . the village. I followed the music. I'm sorry I ruined your song. I didn't mean to say anything, it just came out somehow from inside me."

"Ruined my song? Is that what you're afraid of?" Melehono asked. "Why, you didn't ruin it, you finished it! You gave me just the right word! You say it came from inside of you . . . well, that's where all music comes from. I think you're a pretty good singing monkey!"

Rumbi looked up to see Melehono smiling broadly. "Come on," he said. "You can help me some more." He turned and started walking back towards his house.

I helped him with his song! He thinks I'm a singing monkey! Rumbi thought as he hurried after the musician. *Wait a minute . . . does he really think I'm a monkey?* he wondered. He decided he'd ask about that later.

"Now that we have the words and a melody, we need to add a good beat," Melehono said. "Have you ever played the coco-drums?"

Rumbi shook his head. Although he had seen others play the island instrument at the celebrations.

"It's really not that hard. Sit down over there by those," he pointed to a set of coconuts that had been cut in half and joined together with palm leaf string. Tightly stretched across the top was the skin of a Pulu fish. Lying alongside were two carved tiki sticks.

"Just bang on whichever one you feel like as I'm playing. Don't worry about what it sounds like, you'll get the hang of it soon enough."

Melehono started playing the song again. Rumbi picked up the sticks and looked over at the musician. *Does he really want me to do this?* he wondered.

"Go ahead," Melehono said as he played his kikani and nodded.

Rumbi tapped lightly on one of the coco-drums. It made a nutty, woody sound that he recognized from some of the music he'd heard before. He tapped on another. This time the sound was a little lower.

"Keep going, sounding good!" Melehono said.

Rumbi smiled and hit the biggest one, this time a little harder. The deep resonance seemed to echo out over the ocean waves.

"Go for it," Melehono said. "Whack 'em good!"

Rumbi let go of any remaining hesitation and pounded the coco-drums as hard as he could. Soon, he was trying to hit each one in time to the notes Melehono was playing on the kikani. It sounded pretty much like loud noise to him. He knew that soon Melehono would cover his ears and yell for him to stop – but it sure was fun!

"OK, OK, that's enough for now," Melehono said after a few more minutes of watching Rumbi wear himself out. "You're a pretty good little drummer. Maybe with a little practice you can join me in the music of a celebration some time."

Rumbi beamed.

"So, where do you live, little music monkey?" Melehono asked.

"I live with my aunt on the other side of the village," Rumbi replied. "I was going to the beach to play with the waves when I heard the music."

"Play with the waves . . . that's a great way to put it!" Melehono said. "Maybe I'll make a song about that. You could help me with it."

Rumbi couldn't believe what he had just heard. Melehono wanted him to help make a song! What a morning this was turning out to be. Rumbi had felt earlier that it was going to be a big day, but he didn't expect anything like this!

"Well, alright. I can help," he said, shyly looking down at the sand.

"Here's how to do it," Melehono said, "For the next few days, as you are playing in the water and on the beach, look at the things going on around you – the sun on the water, the color of the sand, the sound of the palm trees swaying in the breeze. Then, close your eyes and think of how it all makes you feel. Try to describe it to yourself. Then, you can describe it to me. Together, we'll work on how to bring that feeling to others in a song."

"I can do that! That's the same thing Nanua always tells me to do! Just think of all the things I like and how they make me feel. That's not very hard."

"No, it really isn't," said Melehono. "It's just that most people don't ever take the time to do it. And I guess that's a good thing for me because that's why they like to listen to my music!"

Rumbi was feeling good. He was glad he had followed the music and had the chance to meet the musician. Not only was Melehono very friendly, but he wanted Rumbi to help him with a song! He pictured himself singing with the musician at the next celebration, everyone dancing and clapping along to the song they had made. He couldn't wait!

Rumbi jumped up. "I have to go now," he said. "I need to get started on feeling the song."

Melehono laughed, "Yes, you do. But you don't always have to be on the beach to feel those things. You can carry the song along inside of you no matter where you are. You can always feel the music."

"I'll be back later," Rumbi yelled as he ran down onto the beach. He stopped and turned around. "Oh, and . . . I'm not really a monkey."

Melehono laughed again as he watched Rumbi run. "Go feel the song," he said to himself. "Feel the song as you play with the waves." He knew that with the help of Rumbi's simple words, he would soon have another tune to play at the next celebration.

Rumbi ran down the beach as fast as he could. He was excited about his time with Melehono and had so much energy he decided to race the wind all the way to Lookout Rock. Finally he arrived, out of breath, at the southernmost point on the island.

Lookout Rock poked like a finger out into the sea. Rumbi liked to think it was pointing the way to adventure and always thought of the stories Peule told about far away lands and people. He would climb all the way out to where it dipped into the ocean and pretend he was on a big sailing canoe heading out to discover new islands.

Standing at the edge, Rumbi gazed at the far ocean horizon. *What is out there?* he wondered. He imagined another island far away with funny birds and tiny little people. *Someday, I'll go there*, he thought. Just then, a big wave crashed into the rocks, throwing salty ocean spray high in the air. Rumbi watched the drops fly into the sky, glistening like shooting stars. He closed his eyes and held up his hands as they showered down on him. "I caught some!" he said to himself looking at his little wet hands. "Now I've got starlight power!"

He looked back out across the ocean just in time to see a little fish jump out of the water and plop back down into the waves. *Maybe he was trying to catch the stars too*, Rumbi thought. *Hmmm . . . Maybe I should go fishing. Nanua always likes it when someone gives her a good fish to cook over the fire.* Rumbi had never been fishing but had often watched as the villagers paddled into the harbor with nets full of sparkling fish.

"Someday, when you are a little older, you'll do that too," his grandmother had told him.

Well, Rumbi thought, *I'm older now. I think it's time for me to go fishing!*

He looked out to the ocean again and said, "I bet there are a bunch of big fish just waiting for my net. I need to get them before it gets too late and they decide to swim away and take a nap."

Rumbi turned and began to climb back towards the beach. Another big wave pounded against the rocks with a deep rumble. He hesitated, feeling a touch of fear. It sounded like the ocean was growling. It was the sound the ocean made during storms when the wind was blowing and the waves were angry. He remembered Makena always said that was the way the ocean warned us to stay safely on the island. He turned and looked out across the water. *But there's no storm now*, he thought. *The waves are friendly today, aren't they?* For a moment, Rumbi thought that maybe he shouldn't go fishing. The ocean did look very big. It could easily swallow a little canoe. Maybe he should just stay on the safe beach.

"I'm not a baby," he said to the waves. "I'm brave. I know I can catch a fish. And besides, I've got extra star power today!" With that, Rumbi overcame his momentary fear and hopped off Lookout Rock to go find a canoe.

❊ ❊ ❊ ❊ ❊ ❊ ❊

Rumbi ran all the way back to his house. He burst through the door to be greeted with a loud "squaaack" from Polo.

"I don't have time to talk now," Rumbi said. "I'm going fishing!"

He peeked out the back door at Anate, who was busy working her clay to make a new pot. Rumbi always thought his aunt made the prettiest containers on the island and he liked to watch her work. Today, though, he had other things on his mind.

"Don't tell her what I'm doing," Rumbi said to Polo. "I want to surprise her and Nanua when I bring back a big fish."

Rumbi put a few more pieces of fruit into his pouch and headed towards the door. He spotted his lucky rock sitting on a table under the window and decided to take that too. *This will help me find the best fish*, he thought.

"Squaaack," said Polo again.

"Do you want to come too?" Rumbi asked. "I guess you could help me find the fish. Let's go." Rumbi held out his arm for Polo to jump onto. "Besides, if you're with me you won't tell anyone where I went!"

As Rumbi ran back down the trail towards the harbor, he glanced back. *Tonight, we'll all be eating the fish I caught*, he thought. He caught a glimpse of his aunt as she walked across the backyard into the house, carrying her pot. For a moment, Rumbi thought about going back to tell her where he was going. *What if I get lost on the ocean? Nobody will know where I am*, he thought. But the excitement of the adventure was too great, so he turned and continued toward the harbor.

Arriving at the harbor, Rumbi paused to watch the activity. He remembered the many times he had stood in this spot in the past, wishing he could be a part of things. He had often watched the fishermen leave in the morning and had imagined the excitement they must feel as they set out for another day on the ocean. Today he was going to join them. *How lucky they are*, he thought. *They get to do something fun every day.*

"It must make them feel good to be helping others like they do," Rumbi said to Polo.

"Squaaack," said Polo. He had been to the harbor before too, usually sitting on Rumbi's shoulder. He had also watched the fishermen leave in the morning and return in the afternoon. He saw how, on some days, the other villagers would greet them with great excitement. He liked to look at the smiles on everyone's faces. But other days, when the nets weren't as full, he had seen how the villagers were not as happy. And sometimes, even when the fishermen brought home many fish, the others would just take them without any thanks and head back to the village center to cook. On those days, the fishermen would grumble about how hard their job was and how no one appreciated them. Polo didn't really understand what anyone was saying, but somehow he could sense that no one was very happy then. On those days, he would look at the bright flowers in the hibiscus bushes instead.

Since it was late in the morning, most of the fishermen had already loaded their canoes and headed out to sea. Rumbi saw there were only a few of the outrigger vessels left on the beach. He walked across the sand towards a smaller one on the end.

"I think this is the best one for us. What do you think Polo?" Rumbi said.

Polo pumped his head up and down, his whole body moving too. Rumbi laughed. He loved it when Polo did this. It made him look like he was agreeing and dancing at the same time.

"All right then, this one it is!"

Rumbi picked up a net lying nearby and threw it into the canoe. He put his pouch of food and lucky rock in the front and said, "Go ahead and get in. Let's get going."

Polo hopped onto the curved front bow as Rumbi began to push the canoe across the sand. Once into the shallow water, he turned the boat around so the front was pointed out towards the harbor entrance. Struggling, he climbed over the edge and plopped in.

"Squaaack!" said Polo as the canoe rocked back and forth.

"Quiet! We don't want anyone to think we're not fishermen too," Rumbi said as he sat up on the seat and picked up the paddle.

Rumbi had been in a canoe only a few other times. Always with Nanua or Anate. They had never gone out very far, always staying in the harbor where the water was calm. Occasionally, they had let Rumbi paddle. His little arms would try to pull the big, carved stick through the water, but the canoe would barely move. They had always instructed him on the proper way to hold the paddle and encouraged him to keep trying. They knew that someday he would be much stronger and would be expected to contribute to the fishing like the other villagers.

Rumbi tried to remember those lessons now as he dipped the paddle into the water and pulled hard. The canoe barely moved. *What's wrong?* he thought, *doesn't this thing work?* He looked over the side and noticed the flat part of the paddle was turned the wrong way. Twisting it around a little, he tried again. This time the canoe moved forward.

"Here we go!" Rumbi shouted as they were off through the waves. "We're going to catch the biggest fish Nanua has ever seen!"

"Squaaack," Polo said as he again did his whole-body head pump.

Rumbi paddled out towards the harbor entrance. The waves were still gentle in the shallow inlet and he could easily see the white sand on the ocean bottom through the clear water.

"Look at the starfish," Rumbi shouted, pointing over the side of the canoe. "They are waving at us!"

Still ahead, Rumbi could see a vast expanse of ocean. "That's where we want to go," he said to Polo.

Polo looked out to where Rumbi pointed. To him, the waves out there looked very big, much bigger than the little canoe they were in. Turning around on the bow, he looked past Rumbi to the shore they had left a little bit ago. From where they were now, it looked very small, a long way away. Polo didn't know much about fishing, but he did know that the beach looked a lot more friendly than the big waves.

Rumbi paddled towards the reef that marked the barrier between the open sea and the port of Alumanaya. By now, the sun was high overhead and bright on the rolling water. The waves crashing over the reef exploded into the blue sky like they had done when he was standing on Lookout Rock, only with much more force. Out here, the water seemed a lot more active and a little scary. Rumbi paused as he watched another big wave pound over the jagged reef.

"I guess we need to go out further to get to where the fish are," Rumbi said to Polo who was nervously pacing on the bow.

Rumbi looked for the opening where his canoe could move safely through the dangerous rocks. He had heard the fisherman talk about this break in the reef that allowed them to get to the fishing grounds. There it was! Just ahead and to his left was where he wanted to be.

"Here we go," he said as he paddled hard towards the opening and the ocean beyond.

As they approached the gap, the canoe started to move much faster. He was paddling hard, but the canoe seemed to be moving on it's own, hurtling towards the sharp coral and crashing waves.

"We're in a rip current!" Rumbi shouted. "It's taking us right into the reef!"

Rumbi had heard the islanders talk of these currents and how they could dash a canoe against the sharp rocks, reducing it to splinters.

"Hold on, Polo!" Rumbi cried as he closed his eyes and gripped both sides of the boat. A big wave picked up the little canoe and threw it towards the reef. They were moving so fast, it felt like they were flying over the water. The roar of the waves was deafening as Rumbi tensed for the impact on the rocks. Suddenly . . . the canoe slowed down. The bellow of the waves faded. Rumbi slowly opened one eye and saw calm waters stretching out as far as he could see. He snapped around to see the waves still crashing against the reef, now behind them. The rip current had hurled the canoe right through the opening! They were safe!

"Polo, we made it!" Rumbi cried. "We're OK! Polo? Polo, where are you?" *Oh no!* Rumbi thought, *Polo fell out in the rough water!*

Then, Rumbi heard a muffled "squaaack" from somewhere in the canoe.

"Polo?" Rumbi said as he began pulling at the fishing net bunched up on the bottom of the canoe. Finally, Rumbi saw a flash of bright color. "There you are," he said, flopping over a fold of the net to uncover a very wet, and a little dizzy, bird.

"For a minute, I thought you had gone overboard," Rumbi said as he smoothed Polo's feathers. "Good thing we had the net in here. If I don't catch any fish, at least I can say I caught a parrot!"

Rumbi looked out over the ocean. The calm, gently rolling water was deep blue. Looking over his shoulder, he saw that the reef was growing smaller behind them. He could also see much more of the island, extending on each side of the harbor. He had never been out this far. Rumbi felt like a real fisherman.

"Let's go out just a little further, then we can throw out the net," Rumbi said as he picked up the paddle.

Polo, back on his perch on the bow, looked out over the water and thought they were out quite far enough, thank you, but what could he do? He was just along for the ride. He started to issue a squaaack of protest, but was distracted by a passing seabird. He forgot about his concern and remained silent.

After a little more paddling, Rumbi decided it was time to fish. Gathering up the net, he began pushing it over the edge.

"There," he said when all but the catch rope was over the side. "Now, all we have to do is wait for the fish to swim into it."

Rumbi looked over at the island as they slowly drifted along the coast. He could see the hills as they turned into mountains, growing up into Kapa Ohono, the volcano in the center of the island. Today, as on most days, the top was covered in clouds. That was another place Rumbi had never been. He had heard many stories about what it was like high on the volcano – how the crater would occasionally spew fire and hot rocks, lighting up the night. To Rumbi, the towering mountain always seemed like another world – filled with croaking and screeching sounds, dripping swirling mists and thick jungle growth. He always thought of the volcano with a mixture of fear and curiosity.

Maybe I'll climb up there next, he thought, thinking of the mysteries that must be concealed in the clouds. *Now that I'm a brave fisherman, I can go anywhere.*

Rumbi lay back in the canoe. A few feathery clouds decorated the deep blue sky. He thought one of them looked like a gecko. He closed his eyes. The warm sun and gentle rocking of the water felt good. *I love it out here*, he thought. *I think I'll go fishing everyday.* He imagined returning each afternoon with his net full, the other villagers crowding around to admire his skill in always finding the biggest fish. He was smiling as he drifted off to sleep.

Polo paced on the bow. He looked at Rumbi sleeping in the canoe, then up at the island they were drifting past. He didn't know how far they had come, where they were going or even what they were doing out here. He only knew that the open water was unfamiliar – much different from the cozy trees and bushes on the island. Polo didn't know or care about adventure, he was ready to go home. And home was getting further away by the minute.

🌴 🌴 🌴 🌴 🌴 🌴 🌴

A strong breeze blew Rumbi's hair, tickling his nose. Slowly waking up, he opened his eyes and sat up in the canoe.

"I guess I took a little nap," he said to Polo who looked back at him from the bow. A stiff wind was blowing Polo's feathers, fluffing him up. Rumbi looked out over the ocean. The waves were much bigger now and far off on the horizon he could see dark clouds crawling across the sky. Behind him, the sun was low, almost touching the water.

Picking up the paddle, Rumbi said, "I must have slept for a long time. We had better get back. It will be dark soon." He turned to look at the island and . . . wait, where was the island? Rumbi stood up in the canoe, struggling to keep his balance in the rough waves. *Is that it, way off in the distance?* he thought. *How could it have gotten so small?*

"Polo!" Rumbi cried, "Is that our island?"

"Squaaack," said Polo. He had watched the island slowly grow smaller as Rumbi slept. He had not thought much about what that meant. Polo didn't understand the ocean currents that were taking them further out to sea.

Rumbi sat down in the canoe.

"We have to get going," he said. "I don't want to be out on the ocean after dark!"

He picked up the paddle and frantically thrashed at the water, trying to turn the canoe around. Rumbi paddled as hard as he could towards the small speck of land, but the canoe barely moved. *Why aren't we going anywhere?* he thought in a panic. He put his head down and paddled with all his strength. When he looked up, he saw the island looked even smaller. The current was carrying them away!

The waves continued to grow. The little canoe bobbed up and down as great hills of water shifted and frothed beneath them. Only the long bamboo outrigger kept them from tumbling over. Rumbi was scared. No matter how hard he paddled, they were moving further and further from the island. He could now only see the island when the canoe rode up to the top of a big wave. It was just barely visible in the distance. The dark clouds, which a few minutes ago had seemed so far away, were now almost overhead, turning the sky into a dark mirror of the churning ocean waters. The wind was much stronger too and was blowing the sun into the sea. Night was falling.

"Polo, what are we going to do? HELP! NANUA! ANATE!" Rumbi shouted as loud as he could. His little voice was carried off in the wind.

Rumbi huddled in the bottom of the canoe and hugged his knees tightly against his chest. "All I wanted to do was catch a fish," he said as his eyes filled with tears. "Now I'm lost on the ocean and it looks like a punamu is coming! I want to go home!"

Polo hopped off the bow and waddled towards Rumbi. Pecking at Rumbi's toes, he tried to help him feel better. Polo didn't know why, but he wasn't scared. Somehow, he knew they would be all right. He wanted Rumbi to know that too. He wanted to say, *Don't worry, it will be OK.* "Squaaack," he said instead.

"At least you're here with me," said Rumbi, wiping his eyes. He stroked Polo's feathers. "Maybe we'll still get home. We'll try to find a way."

Polo was happy to see Rumbi felt a little better. Maybe Rumbi had understood him after all.

As the darkness closed in, Rumbi remembered the fishing net that was still hanging over the edge. Grabbing the catch rope, he struggled to pull it up, hand over hand, until it lay in a heap on the bottom of the canoe. It was empty. *I didn't even catch any fish*, Rumbi thought, shaking his head. *Why did I come out here?* He sat back down and rested his chin on his knees.

Wait . . . did something just move in the net?

He carefully worked through the tangled folds and . . . yes, there it was, a small fish!

"Polo! I caught something!" Rumbi said.

He carefully picked the fish up.

"You're my first catch!" he said. "Even though you're not very big, at least I know I'm a fisherman after all."

Rumbi looked closely at the quivering sliver in his hands. The last of the day's light reflected off of its rounded eyes. At that moment, Rumbi remembered something Makena had said about light and life and realized the little fish was probably as scared as he was.

"You probably want to go home too," Rumbi said to the little fish. "Do you have a Nanua waiting for you like I do?"

Rumbi thought for a minute about what he should do. This was his first catch and he wanted to show it to someone. But somehow he thought of the fish as kind of like him – in a scary place, not knowing what was going to happen next.

"If I let you go, will you tell some of your friends to jump into my net next time?" Rumbi said.

The fish's mouthed moved in what Rumbi took to mean a yes. He smiled. "OK then, it's time for you to go home."

He leaned over the edge of the canoe and gently placed the fish back in the water. It paused for an instant then darted off in the waves.

"I had to let him go," Rumbi said to Polo. "He was late getting home and I didn't want him to get in trouble. Now, when we get home too, you need to make sure you tell Nanua and Anate that I really did catch a fish."

"Squaaack," said Polo. Even though they were still out in a canoe in the stormy ocean, he could feel that Rumbi was happy. Rumbi's ability to think about something good, at least for a moment, made him feel better too.

The light was now gone. The wind was howling and drenching them in cold spray. The churning waves were tossing the little canoe up and down. The storm was increasing it's fury.

"What do we do now?" Rumbi asked, "Where will the ocean take us? Maybe we'll never see the island again!"

A large wave crashed against the canoe, tossing Rumbi to one side. He rolled over on top of the pouch of food he had brought with him. Even though he wasn't very hungry, he thought Polo probably was. He thought they might as well eat.

Rumbi found a mango and took a big bite. The sweet juice running down his chin reminded him of the garden in front of Nanua's house where he often ate breakfast. He closed his eyes. In his mind he could see the sunlight flickering through the swaying palm trees. He imagined he felt the warmth on his skin. He could smell the scent and see the bright colors of the tropical flowers. He could hear Nanua's soothing voice asking him what he was going to do today. Rumbi smiled and opened his eyes. Suddenly, he was right back in the darkness of the storm, the wind and waves as rough as ever.

"Here Polo," Rumbi held out a piece of mango in his hand. "You need to eat too."

As the parrot pecked at the fruit, Rumbi thought of what had just happened.

I thought about Nanua's garden and it almost felt like I was there, he thought. *I wasn't scared. It felt like the storm was gone and I was happy and safe. How could that be?* He was still in his canoe, way out on the stormy ocean, but for a moment he had been somewhere else. He remembered thinking of Makena's voice. How it had calmed him. He loved listening to her tell him about the people of the island and . . . wait, what were those things she had recently told him? About the journey and the ways the people of Alumanaya lived through the difficult times in their lives? Rumbi closed his eyes again and tried to remember his Nanua's words.

"Remember, Rumbi," she had said, "the wind is like life. It is always blowing, just as life is always happening. Sometimes, when the storms of life blow hard, things seem very difficult and scary. Remember to breathe in only what you need. Let the rest blow past you. The winds will soon turn into gentle breezes."

Is this what she was talking about? Rumbi wondered. *Right now, the wind really is blowing and things are scary. Should I do what she said?* He closed his eyes and took a slow, deep breath. He imagined only gentle air flowing into him while the wild punamu storm winds flowed on by, carrying his troubles past him. He concentrated on taking in only what he needed from life right now. After thinking about that for a moment, he opened his eyes. Even though he was still in the storm, he did feel a little better.

As Rumbi and Polo finished the rest of the food, Rumbi thought about the other things Makena had said, about how the sand was like his thoughts. *Well,* he thought, *my thoughts are certainly being blown around now, just like the wind blowing the sand on the beach.* He remembered the idea of his body being like a palm tree bending in the wind and thought of how a little bit ago the stormy waves had knocked him over in the canoe. *Maybe all I can do right now is be flexible and bend with the storm,* he thought.

Remembering these things made Rumbi feel even better.

"Polo," he said, looking down at his parrot, "I don't know where this storm will take us, but if we try to remember what Nanua said, maybe the trip will be a little better."

"Squaaack," said Polo. He didn't know what Rumbi meant, but liked feeling that his friend was not as scared as he had been before.

Rumbi lay down in the bottom of the canoe and pulled the fishing net over him. Polo pressed in against his side.

"We'll be OK, Polo," Rumbi said as he stroked the bird's feathers.

Rumbi closed his eyes and thought again of Makena's words. He remembered the day she had asked him to think of the things he liked about the island and decided to do that now. In his mind, he pictured himself playing on his favorite beach. He could feel the warm sand cuddling his toes. Thinking of the ocean, he saw the sunlight flashing off the calm, rolling water. He could almost hear the soft tumble of the waves as they splashed up the beach. He cupped his hand and held it to his ear. Yes! There it was, the soothing sound of the sea. He thought about how, way down deep, the ocean was calm and peaceful – it was the same somewhere deep inside of him. He took another slow breath and imagined the sweet jasmine scent of a calm island breeze. The fishing net covering him turned into a hammock in the shade of the palm grove by the beach. The tossing of the canoe was instead gentle rocking, coaxing him into pleasant dreams. He drifted off to sleep as the whistling of the storm wind dissolved into the music of Melehono at another happy island celebration.

Polo slept too. He didn't think of any of the things Rumbi did – things from the past or what might happen in the future. He just knew his belly was full of fruit and he was warm huddled next to Rumbi. That was enough for a parrot.

"*Light is everywhere.*"

- Rumbi

Much later, the storm started to die down. A few stars began to peek out from the behind the clouds. As Rumbi slept, he didn't feel the waves and wind slow. But he did feel the canoe suddenly move as something bumped it from below.

Slowly coming out of his dreams, Rumbi felt it again. Something was tapping on the side of the boat.

"Polo, wake up. Did you feel that?" he said. "What was it?"

Rumbi peeked out from under the fishing net. The wind wasn't blowing much now and the waves were much smaller. The storm had moved past. But what was making that noise? And, it seemed like the canoe was moving. Not just randomly with the waves, but in a definite direction.

Maybe I'm still dreaming, Rumbi thought.

But . . . there it was again! Towards the back of the canoe!

Rumbi crawled out from under the net. He slowly peeked over the edge and came face-to-face with a big green sea turtle!

"Whoa!" said Rumbi, jumping back, tumbling over the net.

"Squaaack!" Polo said loudly as Rumbi almost landed on him.

Rumbi had seen sea turtles many times before, but not nearly this close. The surprise of almost touching noses made his heart pound.

"Polo!" he said, "There's a giant turtle trying to get into the canoe!"

Rumbi cautiously leaned over to take another look. The turtle was still there, looking back at him. Then, as Rumbi watched, the turtle dipped his head back in the water and, with a bump, began pushing the canoe. "That is what's making the sound," he said. "The turtle is pushing us."

Rumbi moved closer to the side and peered over again. The turtle picked up his head to look back at him. For some reason, this time Rumbi wasn't scared. As he looked into the turtle's eyes he sensed that this wild ocean creature was friendly and was trying to help them. Rumbi watched as the turtle ducked back into the water and began to push the canoe again, the powerful fins creating a small wake behind them. Rumbi sat back down on the net. *Now what is happening? Where is the turtle taking us?* he wondered.

Rumbi looked up to see more and more stars appearing as the clouds moved off in the distance, carrying the storm with them. Off on the horizon he could see a faint glow. *What is that?* he wondered. He watched as it brightened until a sliver of brilliant white light popped out of the sea. It was the moon! As it slowly rose, it scattered glistening silver-white light across the waters. *Just like Nanua said, light is everywhere*, he thought.

Rumbi looked back at the turtle. Once again, the turtle raised its head out of the water. The moonlight reflected off its eyes and Rumbi thought it almost seemed to be smiling!

"Polo," said Rumbi, "I don't know where the sea turtle is taking us, but I guess there's not much we can do about it. We might as well just go along for the ride. I hope it is pushing us in the right direction."

Rumbi leaned back on the net and looked up at the stars. Even with the bright moonlight, the sparkling pinpoints filled the sky. He thought of how he liked to lay on the beach and look up to the heavens. He could almost hear the voice of Makena pointing out the various shapes the stars made as they drifted across the dark canvas. There . . . he could see the gecko. And over there was Orana, the island hunter. Seeing the familiar shapes in the sky made Rumbi feel better. *Maybe I'm not so far from the island after all*, he thought. The ocean breeze was warm now that the storm had passed. It flowed over his skin, covering him like a soft tropical blanket. Rumbi closed his eyes and felt the canoe moving smoothly through the water. The occasional bump of the sea turtle reassured him. As he fell asleep again, he imagined he saw a shooting star flair across the sky. He told himself it was leading them home.

Polo was watching the turtle when he saw a bright streak above. He turned to look quickly at Rumbi, but saw he was asleep. Polo didn't know what to think about any of this, so he didn't even try. The storm was gone, so he could sit up on the back of the canoe without falling off. Behind him in the water, the sea turtle was steadily pushing them along. The breeze that had helped to put Rumbi to sleep also carried the faint scent of jasmine. To Polo, that meant the garden at Makena's house where he liked to sit in the sun. With that one thought, Polo settled back onto his perch and looked at the big bright moon.

"Little one, little one, wake up." In his dream, Rumbi could hear a voice. He also felt a soft hand shaking his shoulder.

Rumbi opened his eyes to see what looked like the blurry form of a woman leaning over the canoe. The bright sunlight behind her head made it hard to see her face and created a glow around her flowing dark hair.

"Are you an angel?" he asked.

"No," she laughed, "I'm not an angel, but on a beautiful day like today, it's not hard to think you're in heaven!"

Rumbi sat up and looked around. He was on a beach. The canoe was resting on the sand at the edge of the water. The sun was high in the bright blue sky.

"Where am I? Who are you?" Rumbi asked.

"Why, I'm Miri. Who are you?"

"My name is Rumbi. This is Polo," he said, pointing to his friend.

"Well, Rumbi, I don't usually find little boys and parrots sleeping in canoes on this beach. Where did you come from?"

"I came from an island far away. I was out fishing and got caught in a storm. Somehow, I ended up here." Rumbi decided not to tell her about the big green sea turtle. He really wasn't sure there had even been a turtle. Maybe that had just been a dream.

He looked at Miri. She kind of looked like his Nanua, only a little younger. She was wrapped in a loose, multi-colored dress that reached all the way to her bare feet. Around her neck was a string of shells. Over her shoulder, she carried a big bag, painted in more bright colors. She seemed to radiate happiness. Right away, Rumbi felt good just being close to her.

"You came from an island far away you say. Hmmmm," Miri said, frowning in thought as she looked at the canoe. "Well, while we figure out what to do, let's get you something to eat. A fisherman needs to keep up his strength to catch all those big fish."

Rumbi jumped out onto the sand. *She thinks I'm a real fisherman!* he thought.

"Come on, Polo," he said as he reached over for the parrot to hop on his arm.

"I was on my way to my next visit with a neighbor," Miri said, "but I think we can make a short stop to get you some food."

They walked up the beach and into a shady grove of palms. Rumbi saw several mango trees heavy with fruit. Miri picked a mango and tossed it to Rumbi.

"Here's your first course. Let's get you something else." Picking up a stick, she reached up to knock a banana off a stalk. She caught it as it fell.

"Course two," she said, shaking the banana at Rumbi. "Would you like something to wash that down, sir? Some monkey milk perhaps?"

Rumbi laughed. Miri was funny. He liked her.

As Rumbi ate the fruit, he watched Miri move around the palm grove. She almost seemed to float as she bent to smell a flower. She was softly singing a tune Rumbi thought he had heard before.

"Look at the beautiful colors on this one," Miri said, brushing a large bloom. It seemed to brighten with her touch. "See how the light blue of the outer petals gradually darkens to a deep violet in the center. That reminds me of the how the color of the ocean is darker the deeper you look."

Rumbi looked up at Miri. *That sounded like something Nanua would say*, he thought. There was something very familiar about Miri, but Rumbi was sure he hadn't met her before . . . had he?

"I see you've finished your fruit. Are you ready to go?" Miri asked.

"Go? Where are we going?" said Rumbi.

"As I said before, I was on my way to check on someone. She isn't feeling well and she's expecting me this morning. Come on, she'll be happy to have additional visitors, especially a cute little fisherman and his fluffy parrot."

Rumbi and Miri walked along the beach until they came to a path leading up into the palms.

"This is the way to her house. She lives up on the hill," Miri said. "She's too sick to come into the village, so we'll come to her."

As they started up the trail, Rumbi looked up at the hills. They were covered with dark green foliage and gradually got bigger the farther he looked. Way off in the distance, there was a mountain that rose up into the clouds. It reminded him of the volcano on his own island. *Where am I?* he wondered.

Soon, a small thatch house appeared.

"Hello!" called Miri. "Are you home?" She pulled the curtain on the door aside as she and Rumbi stepped in. "Good morning, pretty lady! How are you this lovely day?"

"Miri!" Rumbi heard from the corner of the dim house. "There you are."

"Let's get some sunlight in here," Miri said as she rolled up the cloth window shades. "Got to have light to feel better." As the room brightened, Rumbi saw an old woman lying on a bed in the corner.

"I had to put the shades down last night because of the storm," the woman said. "I haven't felt like getting out of bed this morning to open them again. Thank you."

"I have helpers this morning," Miri said. "This is Rumbi, the brave fisherman, and his friend, Polo."

"Well, aren't you a fine looking young man? Come closer so I can see you better," the old woman said, reaching out her hand.

Rumbi slowly walked over to the bed and let her take his hand. Her skin felt dry, like the bark of a fallen palm tree. Rumbi looked into her tired eyes. They seemed as deep as the ocean itself and he started to pull back, a little frightened. She seemed very old and barely alive. But then, the old woman smiled. "It's alright young one, I won't bite. It wouldn't hurt much anyway, since I hardly have any teeth left!"

Rumbi relaxed a little and sat down by the bed. He couldn't think of anything to say.

"Let's see how you're doing this morning," Miri said as she sat down next to Rumbi.

She placed her hand on the woman's forehead. "Your temperature feels fine. Just the right amount of heat."

Next, Miri pulled something out of her bag. To Rumbi, it looked like two small shells joined by woven cord. He watched Miri hold one shell up to her ear and put the other one on the woman's chest. She listened for a moment.

"Your heartbeat is strong. It sounds like it's keeping time to a happy tune," Miri said as she put the shells away. "How about you go sit at the table so you can take some medicine and eat a little something?" She helped the old woman struggle out of bed and over to a chair. "Rumbi, would you get that bowl over there?" She pointed to a coconut shell sitting on the windowsill.

Rumbi reached for the shell and handed it to Miri. It contained what looked to him like mashed up leaves. Miri picked up a spoon and dipped out a bit of the mixture.

"Here you go," she said, holding the spoon up to the old woman's mouth. "Your favorite! Yummmm!"

The old woman swallowed the leaves and made a face. "I think you're trying to kill me with that stuff," she said. But Rumbi saw she was smiling at Miri.

The old woman reached for a papaya that was sitting in a bowl on the table. "So, where did you come from?" she asked Rumbi as she broke off pieces of the fruit and began to eat. Miri was brushing the woman's long gray hair.

Rumbi looked back at her and was amazed at what he saw. In the short time since they had arrived, the old woman seemed transformed. She appeared to be soaking in the kindness and attention from Miri and was responding like a blooming flower. The darkness he had thought he had seen in her eyes earlier was now replaced with a sparkle.

"I . . . uh, well . . . I came from another island," Rumbi stammered, not knowing how else to describe Alumanaya. "I went out fishing and was caught in a storm. The wind and big waves carried me far away. Then it got dark and I couldn't see the island anymore."

Tears filled Rumbi's eyes as he continued, "All I wanted to do was catch a fish to show my Nanua that I'm a real fisherman. Now I'm somewhere far away and I'll never see her or my Aunt Anate again!"

"You were out in the storm last night?" the old woman asked. "In a canoe?"

"Yes," Rumbi replied. "I tried to be brave, but I was scared. Then I remembered what my Nanua taught me to do when I felt bad – about the wind and breathing in just what you need and how I can always go back home to the island in my mind. So, I thought about the things that make me happy – the waves, the sand, the warm sunlight – and I started to feel a little better. I guess I fell asleep and woke up here in this place this morning."

Upon hearing all this, the old woman turned to Miri with a questioning look. Miri was listening closely to Rumbi and slowly nodding her head. She smiled. She now had a pretty good idea of where Rumbi had come from.

Miri put her arm around Rumbi. "It's OK, Rumbi, you'll see your Nanua and aunt again. I promise. I think I may know how you can get home."

Rumbi sniffled and wiped his eyes. *A brave fisherman never cries!* he thought, wishing he had held back his tears. He was trying to be a big boy, but Miri's hug did feel comforting. And, what was that she said about helping him to get home?

"We had better get going," Miri said. "We've got others yet to see today."

She took the old woman's hands in hers and smiled. "Remember to let the light flow into you. You will be feeling much better soon." Miri closed her eyes for a moment and Rumbi sensed that something was passing from her to the woman.

"I already do," the old woman replied. "Thank you for coming today. You'll come back soon?"

"Yes, I'll be back in a few days," said Miri. "Come on Rumbi, let's go."

Polo hopped on Rumbi's arm as they headed for the door. The old woman got out of her chair, this time on her own, and followed them to the door. As they started down the trail, Rumbi turned to look back at the house. The old woman waved and called, "Next time you visit, Rumbi, I want you to bring me a fine fish!"

Rumbi waved back and thought again how much happier and healthier she looked after the short visit from Miri.

"Where are we going now?" Rumbi asked as they arrived back at the beach.

"We've got a few more people to see, then it will be time to eat dinner. After that, I have a surprise I think you'll like," Miri said.

As they walked, Rumbi struggled with asking Miri about what she had said at the house. He was afraid that maybe he didn't hear her right. Did she really say something about him going home? He looked up at her and thought about how, even though he had only met Miri a little while ago, it seemed like he had known her a long time. He trusted her. She wouldn't make something up just to make him feel better, would she? After all, she had promised he would see his family again.

Miri glanced down at Rumbi. His eyes opened wide as she caught him looking at her.

"So, is there something you would like to say?" she said, smiling at him.

"Well, yes, I, uh . . . well, back at the old woman's house, you said you knew how I can get home. Did you really mean it?"

"Yes, I did. You'll be home again soon enough," Miri said. "But I need to think about that a little more before we talk about it. How about we wait until after dinner, OK?"

"OK," said Rumbi. It *was* true! Miri would help him get home! He started to hop around on the sand, bouncing Polo off his shoulder. He was so excited he ran down to the water, skipping through the shallow waves. Miri ran after him and splashed too, holding her skirt up to her knees. Laughing, they kicked water high into the air, the shining beads falling all around them.

"OK, OK, enough," said Miri, still laughing. "We'll be so wet we'll never get dry! Besides, we have more work to do." After a moment, she added, "But nobody said we can't have a little fun while we work!"

She took Rumbi's hand as they continued their walk down the beach, this time with the frothy waves rolling around their ankles.

Share the light – your own sense of inner joy and strength."

- Miri

Soon they were back to where they had left Rumbi's canoe earlier in the morning.

"This time we're going the other way," said Miri. "See that trail over there?"

Rumbi nodded.

"That takes us back to the village. On the way, there are a few more people we need to see."

As they walked up the trail, a bright green gecko darted into the bushes. It looked just like the ones on Alumanaya. Ahead, Rumbi saw the green hills in the distance and beyond them, the mountain that rose into the clouds. Once again, he thought of how much this place reminded him of his own island home. It felt almost the same, but somehow different. Maybe he would ask Miri about that later.

They arrived at another thatch house. This time, there was an old man sitting out in front carving a piece of wood.

"Hey there, have you seen any good-looking woodcarvers around here?" Miri called from the trail.

"You found one right here!" laughed the old man as he put down his knife. "Come on over here and get a better look."

Miri walked over to him and bent to give him a hug. "Well, aren't you the busy one today? Making another masterpiece, I see."

"Don't know about masterpiece," he said, "but it does keep me busy. Who's this?"

"This is Rumbi. He's helping me today," said Miri.

"Rumbi, huh? Well, Rumbi, I see you have a little friend there." He pointed at Polo, who was sitting on Rumbi's shoulder. "Have you ever seen what happens when a parrot gets really, really old?"

Rumbi shook his head.

"They end up looking like this," he reached behind an old palm tree stump and picked up another carving. It was a small wooden parrot.

"Squaaack!" said Polo, loudly, causing Rumbi to jump.

"Now, don't you be talking that nonsense, scaring little boys and birds," scolded Miri. "Polo is a fine, well-mannered creature, unlike some cranky old woodcarvers I know."

"It's OK," Rumbi said. "I know that parrots don't turn into wood. Polo knows too."

Rumbi was at least pretty sure that Polo wouldn't turn to wood, although the carving did look pretty real.

"You are right, little one. Your bird won't ever look like this, but maybe he'd like a new friend of his own," he handed the little wooden parrot to Rumbi.

"I can have it?" asked Rumbi.

"Yes, take it with you. Everyone, even parrots, can never have too many friends," he said as he looked over at Miri and smiled.

"Thank you," said Rumbi. "Look, Polo, you have a little brother!"

"Squaaack," said Polo. They all laughed as the real, live parrot made a show of turning around on Rumbi's shoulder to ignore the new addition to the family.

Rumbi watched as Miri repeated much of the same procedure with the old man as she had with the old woman. She finished the same way as before, holding his hands in hers for a moment. Rumbi was curious about this last part. *What is she doing?* he wondered.

"Everything looks good," she said. "It looks like you'll be around to aggravate us all for some time to come."

"Well, somebody's got to do it," he replied, winking at Rumbi. "Got to keep things spiced up a bit."

As Miri packed her bag, they talked about what treasures the old man had carved recently. He showed them a good luck tiki he had just finished, explaining to Rumbi what each section of the carvings meant – how it actually told a short story. Miri smiled as she watched the old man talking with Rumbi. She saw how happy he was to have a little student for a while. She knew that much of her life as a Kamua was simply connecting with her patients on a personal basis – showing them that someone cares about them, that they were still an important and needed part of the world. *Isn't it important for us all to know that?* she thought.

"OK, Rumbi, we've got to get going or we'll never make our other stops. This old fellow here will talk your ear off if you let him." Miri stood up and said, "I'll be back in a few days. You take care, and remember the light."

"Thank you for the wooden parrot," Rumbi said.

"You keep him with you, young one. He'll bring you good luck too," the old man said as he picked up his knife and went back to work.

Back out on the trail, Rumbi turned around for a last look at the old man and saw he had paused in his carving.

He was leaning back against his house with his eyes closed. A shaft of sunlight had worked its way through the trees to his face. He was smiling.

I guess he's soaking in the light like Miri said, Rumbi thought. That was something else he meant to ask her about.

They made several more stops where Miri did pretty much the same things as before. She always introduced Rumbi and Polo and talked for a while about things going on in the village. Rumbi saw again and again how much brighter and happier the people seemed to be by the time they left, even though it sometimes didn't seem like Miri did much more than talk with them and hold their hands. *It's almost like she is a good luck tiki herself*, he thought.

It was beginning to seem like a long day. Rumbi was tired. "I'm kind of hungry," he said to Miri, hoping they could rest for a while.

"We're almost finished," she said. "Just one more visit to make. You say you're hungry? Well, I hope so, because tonight there will be more food than you've ever seen! And, you better be ready to dance!" Miri took Rumbi's hand and skipped around in a circle.

Rumbi laughed, "Where are we going tonight?"

"You'll just have to wait and see," Miri said mysteriously. "But I think you'll have fun."

They arrived at their last stop for the day. Rumbi saw that Miri now seemed a little sad. Her ever-present smile was gone.

"You and Polo should wait out here this time," she said. "I'll be back soon."

Walking up to the door of the house, Miri paused for a moment and closed her eyes. She took a deep breath. Rumbi could see her lips moving – she seemed to be talking silently to herself. Then her smile reappeared and she entered the house. He could hear her cheerful voice talking to someone inside.

While he waited, Rumbi thought about the day. He had been so caught up in visiting people with Miri that he had barely thought about his troubles. It was amazing how just yesterday, he had been standing on Lookout Rock, on his own island. While today, he was in a new place, far away. He thought about how, throughout the day, he had been reminded of his home. Things were different here, but somehow the same. *What did that mean?* he wondered. He remembered what Miri had said about him getting home. Did she know where he lived? How could they find their way back across the big ocean? He had no idea which way the wind and waves and taken the little canoe. He thought about other things Miri had said, not only to him, but to the people they had visited – things about light and helping. They sounded like something his Nanua would say. Rumbi hoped that tonight Miri would answer the many questions he had.

Polo sat next to Rumbi, staring out into the tropical forest. He was thinking too, although not about any of the things that were troubling his owner. His gaze was fixed on a macadamia tree that was full of ripe nuts. Polo didn't really care that they were in a strange new place. Any thoughts about what might happen in the future never occurred to him. He just knew that, right now, the sun was warm, the gentle breeze felt good as it tickled his feathers, and that one big fat nut looked really tasty.

Rumbi turned as he heard Miri coming out of the shack. She had said her usual happy goodbye, but as she walked towards him, her smile faded away.

"She isn't doing very well," she said. "I don't know how much longer I'll be coming to visit here."

Miri was quiet as they walked along the trail. Rumbi even thought he could see Miri's eyes glistening with tears. This last visit had really upset her. All day, Rumbi had watched Miri make others feel better. Now, it seemed she needed encouragement too, but what could he do? He couldn't think of anything to say, so he reached out and took her hand.

"Thank you," Miri said.

Looking up, Rumbi saw a faint smile begin to appear. He had helped! That made him feel very good. In fact, it was the best feeling he'd had all day.

Soon, they came to another house on a small hill. It was surrounded by lush green bushes and bright, multi-colored flowers.

"Here we are, home at last," Miri said. "Let's go in and get a little something to eat. But we can't eat much, we don't want to spoil our appetite for later."

"Where are we going later?" Rumbi asked.

"You'll see soon enough," Miri said.

Rumbi fidgeted. He was ready to know now!

Inside, there were almost as many flowers as there were outside. The late afternoon sun filtered in through the window and lit up colorful woven hangings that decorated the walls. The small hut did feel like home, even to Rumbi.

"Go ahead and eat a piece of fruit," said Miri, pointing to the bowl on the table. "You can sprinkle some coconut flakes on it if you want. Polo probably wants a little too.

Oh, he may like these even better," she picked up a small bowl and handed it to Rumbi. It was full of macadamia nuts.

"Squaaack!" said Polo. He had been thinking about nuts since they left the last house.

"Go on outside to eat. You can see the gathering area of the village from there," Miri said.

Rumbi took the fruit and nuts and went out to sit on a stump in front of the house. From there he could see a number of houses clustered around a large open space. There was a lot of activity. People were scurrying about setting up tables and decorations.

What are they doing? Rumbi wondered. It looked a little like . . . yes! It looked like they were preparing for a celebration!

"Miri!" Rumbi called, jumping up. "Is that where we are going? Is there a party tonight?"

He turned to run back into the house and ran right into Miri as she came out the door.

"Yes, that's the surprise!" she said. "Tonight is very special. It's the first night of the sea turtle homecoming. We always celebrate them coming back to our beach."

Rumbi had heard about this before. He had listened as the elders of his own village told about how the sea turtles would come ashore every year to lay their eggs in the sand. Then, a few weeks later, the little turtles would break through the shells and scurry back into the sea. But this never happened on Rumbi's own beach. The elders said it only occurred in a special area of the island, a place far away. Rumbi had always wondered where that faraway place was. Was this it?

"There will be a lot of good food. That's why I didn't want you to eat too much now. We need to go a little early to help with the decorations. Are you both ready?" Miri asked.

"Yes! Lets go!" Rumbi said.

"Squaaack!" said Polo, hopping up and down.

"One more thing," Miri said. "We need to get in the proper spirit. Here, put this on." She handed Rumbi a beautiful flower lei. She already had one around her neck. "Now, lets do a quick party dance." She raised her hands in the air and wiggled her whole body. "Ooooooh, it's time for fun!"

Rumbi laughed. Miri looked silly.

"Come on, you have to do it too. Raise your hands, twist and jiggle."

126

Rumbi did what Miri did, shouting with her, "Oooooh, it's time for fun!"

They were both laughing now. It did feel good! Rumbi was now ready for the celebration.

"OK, lets go," she said as they headed towards the activity.

"Notice and appreciate all the beautiful colors of life."

- Miri

As they were helping to decorate, Miri introduced Rumbi to everyone. They all told him how happy they were that he was there. Rumbi was happy to be there too, he just wished his Nanua, Anate and his friends from his island could be there as well.

There were long tables filling up with food. Rumbi saw big plates of baked sweet potatoes wrapped in Noni leaves. Steaming bowls of poi, pounded from taro root, sat next to breadfruit and lemon-seasoned sea grass. There was more fruit than he had ever seen in one place, including one of his favorite treats, sweet mountain apples. At one end of the clearing was a big fire where several villagers were roasting pork and fresh fish over the hot coals. This was truly a feast!

As more and more people appeared, the excitement grew. The sun was falling behind the mountain when Rumbi heard a long, deep bellow from a big conch shell. Everyone quieted down and turned to look at a man who was standing on a stump close to the center of the clearing. He wore a necklace made of shark's teeth.

That must be the leader of the village, Rumbi thought.

"Brothers and sisters," he began, "welcome to the celebration of the sea turtles. Once again, we gather to welcome back our friends from the far waters and to bless their eggs. In doing this, we bless ourselves as well, for we are reminded that not only is life continually renewing, but everything is connected and united in spirit. Tonight, celebrate the sea turtles, but always, always, celebrate life itself."

With that, a cheer went up and the party began!

. Rumbi and Miri soon had big plates of food and Polo had more macadamia nuts to gnaw on. As they sat at one of the big tables, Rumbi listened as the villagers talked about things that had happened to them recently and their upcoming plans. It reminded him of the talk he had heard at the celebrations he had been to before. These people seemed to be just like the people of his own village. They had the same concerns and hopes, and, dressed in their bright cloth wraps and flowered leis, they even looked pretty much the same. Rumbi almost felt like he was home.

Rumbi was finishing the last bites on his plate when the first notes of music filled the air. Clapping began as a voice began singing,

"We come to laugh, we come to sing.
We come to remember we have everything.
Forget our worries, there's none we see.
Come on people and dance with me."

The villagers streamed into the open area in front of the music stand. Rumbi couldn't see who was playing, but thought the music sounded very familiar. He even thought he had heard this song before – at a celebration on his own island. In fact, he thought it sounded a lot like Melehono!

Miri jumped up, "Come on, Rumbi, let's dance."

She took Rumbi by the hand and pulled him out into the crowd. It seemed like almost everyone at the celebration was in the clearing, moving to the smooth island rhythm. Rumbi loved to dance and was soon trying to follow what Miri was doing. He liked watching her. She moved around the dance area like a feather floating on the currents of the music. He followed, hopping and twisting in his own little-boy way.

"Isn't this fun!" Miri said. "Feel the music in here." She touched him lightly on the chest.

That reminded Rumbi of how Makena had told him to feel things in his heart.

They moved around the dance area until they were close to the source of the music. Rumbi tried to look between the dancing villagers to see who was playing. He still thought the song sounded like something he had heard before – like something Melehono would play. Just then, the music stopped and everyone paused. Rumbi moved a few steps closer to see who was singing.

"He sounds like Melehono, the one who plays music at the celebrations on my island," Rumbi said, turning to Miri.

"Yes, he does," Miri said. "Sometimes he and Melehono sing together."

"How can they do that?" Rumbi said. "Melehono lives on my island."

"I know. He lives on my island too," Miri said.

Now Rumbi was really confused. *How can Melehono live in two places at once?* he thought.

Seeing Rumbi's perplexed look, Miri smiled and said, "Remember how earlier today I said I had an idea about how you can get home?"

Rumbi nodded.

"Well, Rumbi, you *are* home." Looking up at the musician, Miri said, "Why don't you tell him exactly where we are?"

He began to sing,

"Seeking adventure, how far I have sailed.
Testing my courage,
sometimes thinking I've failed.
But the sun shines this morning,
never more I will roam.
I'll stay here on Alumanaya,
my island home.
Yes, I'm living Alumanaya,
my island home."

"Come on, Rumbi," said Miri, taking him by the hand. "Let's go sit down and talk."

She waved to the musician who was continuing the song. As they made their way through the dancing villagers, Rumbi could hear them singing along with him.

Back at their table, Miri explained, "You see, Rumbi, when I came upon you this morning, I wondered how such a small boy, even with his parrot friend, could have traveled very far across the big ocean, especially in the storm. I also recognized your canoe. It was made in the same way as the others on the island. Then, as we talked throughout the day, you mentioned several things that confirmed where you were from.

"Remember how you said your Nanua told you to breathe in and take only what you need from the wind, and how that helped you feel better?" she asked.

Rumbi nodded.

"Well, long ago, I was taught to do that too, by the same person who taught you. Your Nanua is Makena, isn't it?"

"Yes! Do you know her?" Rumbi asked.

"I do. She was my also my teacher. I was about your age when she told me about the ways of the people of our island – how the ocean, wind, sand, palm trees and light work together and how we can relate them to our lives."

"But how did you get to this place?" Rumbi asked. "And how is this place the same as my island?"

Miri laughed again, "I know it's a little hard to understand at first, Rumbi. But this place *is* your island. It's just another part. You live on the side where the beach is long and flat and the waves are usually gentle, right?"

Rumbi nodded.

"And, I bet you've climbed all the way out to the edge of Lookout Rock."

"Yes! That's where I decided I wanted to catch a fish!" Rumbi said.

"When I was a little girl, I used to stand on Lookout Rock too, but I didn't want to be a fisherman. That's where I decided I wanted to be a Kamua, a healer. Looking out at the big ocean made me think about how small our island really is and how I wanted to help as many of the others as I could. I guess there have been many little girls and boys, older folks too, who have stood in the same place thinking about what to do with their lives.

"Where you are right now is also part of Alumanaya. It's the other side of the island. Even though things may seem a little different here, it's really just a different part of the same place."

Rumbi thought back to how earlier in the day he had noticed several things that reminded him of home – the the lizard, the trees, and especially the big mountain.

"On my side," Rumbi said, trying to understand, "there is a big mountain that rises up into the clouds. I saw one like that here too."

"That's the same mountain, Kapa Ohono. Although it's not really a mountain, it's a volcano. You're seeing the other side of it," Miri said.

"So, if we're on the same island, it's easy for me to go home," Rumbi said.

"Well, it's a long way back to the other side, but you're right, it's not so far to where you can't get back. The question is, how are we going to do that? How are we going to get you home? It's too far to paddle your little canoe, so that's not a good idea. Besides, I'm not going to send a little boy and a parrot off on their own."

"But then, how am I going to get home?" Rumbi asked. He was starting to worry that he would be staying here. Even though he liked Miri very much, he still wanted to go home.

"There is another way, but it's very difficult. I'm not sure what to do. I want to think about it for a while," Miri said.

Just then, another long note from the conch shell sounded.

"It's time to go down to the beach to watch the sea turtles," Miri said. "We'll talk more about how to get you home later. Don't worry, Rumbi. Remember, I promised you would see your family again."

Rumbi looked into Miri's smiling eyes and believed her.

R umbi and Miri followed the crowd toward the ocean. The villagers stopped in the trees on the edge of the sand. The full moon was bright on the water and lit up the wide beach.

"Tonight is when the sea turtles start to arrive," Miri said in a quiet voice. "Some of them travel a great distance to get to this spot."

"Why do they always come here?" Rumbi asked.

"Because this is where they were born. Like us, they always feel something special about their home. They come back so their young can start their lives here too."

Rumbi looked out at the waves. All he could see were a few rocks in the shallow water. Where were the turtles? Then he noticed the rocks seemed to be getting bigger. They were moving!

"There are the first ones," Miri said, pointing at what Rumbi had thought were rocks.

They watched as the big green sea turtles slowly crawled out of the waves and up the beach. Well away from the water, the turtles started to dig in the sand, making a nest for their eggs.

"The eggs will stay covered for a few weeks. Then, the baby turtles will hatch and crawl back into the ocean. One day, they too will return here with eggs of their own," Miri said.

After lying very still for a while, the sea turtles replaced the sand they had dug and turned to make their way back to the sea.

"They've buried their eggs. We can get a little closer now," Miri said as they slowly walked towards the turtles.

From only a few feet away, they looked very big. Seawater glistened on their shells and scaly skin as they worked hard to get back to the ocean.

This one looks just like the one I saw last night, Rumbi thought, moving a little closer. *But maybe I didn't see a turtle at all. Maybe it was all just a dream.*

At that moment, the sea turtle turned and looked right at him. The moonlight reflected off its eyes just as Rumbi had remembered from the night before. As Rumbi looked back with his own wide eyes, he thought he saw the sea turtle smile and give a slight nod. *Do sea turtles smile?* he wondered.

"Did you see that?" Rumbi said to Miri. "He looked right at me!"

"Yes, *she* did," Miri said with a smile. "She's a girl turtle, Rumbi. It looks like you have a friend."

Rumbi decided that, dream or not, the sea turtle *had* helped him get back to the island. Maybe she was coming here herself to lay eggs or maybe she just swam in his imagination – either way, he did have a new friend.

Finally, all the sea turtles had disappeared back into the water. Rumbi, Miri and the rest of the villagers made their way back to the clearing. The party was dying down now. Some people remained at the tables, sitting and talking, while others went off to their homes.

"It's getting late, Rumbi," Miri said. "It's time to go home. We've had quite a day, haven't we?"

"Yes," Rumbi mumbled, suddenly finding it hard to keep his eyes open.

"You may need a little help getting to bed. Come on," Miri said as she bent to pick Rumbi up. He locked his arms around her neck and laid his head on her shoulder. Miri had only taken a few steps before he was fast asleep.

As Miri carried Rumbi along the path to her house, she thought again about what to do about getting him home. She knew there was only one real answer – she would take him back to his village. The trip would be long and difficult. They would not go the same way Rumbi had taken to get here. Even though he had been very brave to make it through the storm and wake up in a strange new place, she hoped he was ready for the challenges that would lie ahead. Miri knew Rumbi wanted to think of himself as a brave fisherman, but as she carried her softly snoring bundle through the trees, she knew he was still very much a little boy.

Back at the house, as Miri was laying Rumbi in a hammock by the window, she heard a fluttering of wings.

"Squaaack," said Polo, landing on the window ledge.

"Oh no!" said Miri. "We forgot you, didn't we? Well, I'm glad you followed us home. Did you get enough to eat at the celebration?"

"Squaaack," said Polo again. He didn't have any idea what Miri had just said, but it seemed like she wanted him to say something back. He had eaten so many macadamia nuts he could barely fly and was glad Miri didn't live too far from where the party had been. Settling on a knot at one end of Rumbi's hammock, he closed his eyes and was soon asleep too.

Miri lay down in her hammock and thought about the upcoming trip. She had a lot to do before they left. She wouldn't need to take much food; they would be able to find things to eat along the way. She thought about taking extra clothes and a blanket. The one time she had made this journey before, it had gotten cold at night.

As she worked through what to take, her thoughts turned to her main concern – what she had been wrestling with all day – what to do about her patients? She knew they depended on her not just for the medicine, but for the companionship and uplifting talk she brought with each visit. Could someone else do that? Could she trust them to take care of "her" people the way she did?

Looking out the window, she could see the bright stars through a break in the trees. Soon, her favorite constellation, Orana, came into view. For some reason, seeing the island hunter in the sky always made her feel better. It was something that was always there, a constant she could depend on. She listened to the sounds of the tropical night. The various insects and night birds were having their own celebration.

In the background was the chorus of the ocean waves in the distance, rhythmically washing the beach clean in anticipation of another day. Miri fell asleep trusting that she would be given help in deciding the best thing to do.

Miri awoke to color – the big orange sun peeking through the trees and the big brown eyes of Rumbi looking at her.

"Lets go!" Rumbi said.

"Go? Go where?" Miri said, rubbing her sleepy eyes.

"Back to my side of the island!" said Rumbi. "I've already packed some food and have everything ready. So, lets go."

Miri saw a small bag at Rumbi's feet. She could see a few pieces of fruit inside and knew it probably also contained the carved parrot the old man had given him along with the rock he had brought with him from his own house.

"Not so fast, Mr. Adventure," Miri said, climbing out of her hammock. "We've got a lot to do first. We'll also need to take a few more things with us. But it does look like you're off to a good start!"

After eating breakfast, they went into the village. Rumbi sat on a palm stump and watched the morning activity while Miri talked with several different people. He noticed she spent quite a while with one village woman in particular. She seemed to be explaining something while the woman nodded. Finally, they hugged and Miri started over towards Rumbi.

"Have a good trip," the other villagers called to her, waving. "Remember to live Alumanaya."

"OK, Rumbi," Miri said. "Let's go back to the house and finish packing. Then we'll be on our way."

"What were you talking to the others about?" asked Rumbi.

"I needed to figure out how my patients would be cared for while I am gone," Miri said. "Yesterday, I struggled with that all day. It was bothering me that I might be leaving for a while. I know they depend on me to help them with their healing, especially the last one we visited."

Rumbi remembered how Miri had been upset after leaving that last house.

"Last night, before I went to sleep, I asked for help in deciding the best thing to do," Miri continued. "When I woke up this morning, I had an answer."

"Who told you?" Rumbi asked.

Miri laughed, "I'm not sure I can answer that, but it's someone or something that is part of all of us and is always there to help. All you have to do is ask. I couldn't seem to think of a solution on my own, so I just asked for direction and then listened with my heart for the answer. This morning, I knew what to do. The friend I was talking with for such a long time will visit my patients while I'm gone. She is a Kamua too and I know she will take good care of them."

Back at the house, Miri gathered a few more things and put them in her bag. Looking around, she tried to think of anything else they might need.

"I think we're ready to go," she finally said. "I'll take this bag, you can carry yours. It's easier if we wear them like this." She helped Rumbi adjust his bag to hang on his back.

As they headed for the door, Miri turned around. "Wait, I think we're forgetting someone!" She pointed towards a feathery figure sleeping on his perch.

"Polo!" shouted Rumbi, running over to his parrot.

"Squaaack!" said Polo as he was jolted awake.

Rumbi held out his arm and Polo stepped onto it, quickly climbing up to his shoulder.

Out in front of the house, Miri stopped and said, "Rumbi, we're about to start a journey that will take a while and may be difficult at times. We'll see some things we've never seen before and probably learn a lot more about our island world. It may be a little scary at times, but we'll also have fun along the way. We'll need to always remember and practice the things Makena has taught us. Are you ready to go?"

Rumbi nodded, remembering how Makena had also called her teaching a journey.

"What kind of scary things will there be?" he asked.

"We don't know yet," Miri said, smiling. "That's part of the excitement of starting something new. We never know exactly how things will turn out or what might happen. We just trust that everything will work out the way it is supposed to. We always think of the good things that are ahead. What is it that you are looking forward to the most when you get back to your village?"

Rumbi thought for a moment. "Playing in the waves," he said.

"Well, just think about that from time to time as we go. You will soon be back on your beach, running through the ocean water. It's OK to feel a little scared right now, everybody does when they do something they've never done before. But if we're too scared to even start, we'll never get to where we want to go, will we?"

"No, I guess not," said Rumbi.

"OK then! Let's get you back to your friends, the waves!" said Miri.

146

They took a few steps to the trail where Miri turned one way and Rumbi turned the other.

"Miri, it's this way to the beach and the canoe," Rumbi said.

"I know, but that's not the way we are going," Miri replied. "The ocean currents and trade winds make it very difficult to travel to the other side by water. Besides, your little canoe is too small for both of us anyway. We're going this way, across the island."

Rumbi looked up at the hills. Way off in the distance he could see the big mountain. As always, the top was invisible in the clouds.

"We're going over the volcano?" he asked.

"Yes, that's the main way to get back to the other side of the island. All we have to do is follow the trail."

Rumbi looked again towards the misty peak. It looked very far away. Taking a deep breath, he took Miri's hand and they started towards the other side of the island.

As they walked, Miri tried to imagine the early islanders who had traveled along this path generations ago. As a little girl, she had heard stories about how the early explorers had struggled against the steep mountains that formed a ridge across the center of the island. They had eventually found a passage through the volcanic rock and deep canyons to make it to the windward side. Miri thought of the struggles they must have faced in creating a new settlement and felt grateful for their sacrifices. She appreciated all she and the others had in their village.

She also thought back to the time, years ago, when she had traveled this route for the first time. While the trip itself had seemed long, she remembered that the hardest part had been the inner journey she had also been taking at the same time. At that point, Miri had been very unsure of where life was taking her. She had grown up in the leeward village, the same one where Rumbi now lived. She, too, had learned the ways of her people from Makena.

As a little girl, she had never thought beyond remaining in the village forever, someday marrying and having her own family. She had loved helping her mother work on the colorful wraps that the people of the village often wore at the celebrations. The best part had been when they would give the finished cloth to the person for whom it had been made. The grateful villager would hug them both in thanks and appreciation of their hard work. It always made Miri feel good to think she was helping to make others happy. One day she told her mother that when she grew up, she wanted to be a cloth-maker too.

"There are many ways to bring joy into the world, Miri," her mother had said. "The trick is finding the right one for you."

"How do I find the right way for me?" Miri asked.

"Don't worry, you'll know when you do. Usually, it will find you. Sometimes when and where you least expect it." her mother had said.

Walking along the trail with Rumbi, Miri smiled to herself remembering those happy times with her mother. As a little girl, she had loved her life and remembered how she had thought at the time that things would never change. But they had. Her smile faded away as she recalled how her life had taken one of those unexpected turns.

Miri was in her early teens when her mother got sick. The trouble had come on quickly. It seemed like one day her mother was handing over yet another piece to a happy villager, and the next, she was too weak to work with the fancy cloth.

The rest of the family had all tried to help in the care, but it soon became too much. Her mother was very ill. Miri would watch as the Kamua would come to their house, bringing medicines in little containers. She saw how the healer would always hold her mother's hands for a moment before she left. She also saw how her mother always felt better after the visit and would look forward to seeing the Kamua again.

One day, as the healer was leaving, Miri followed her out of the house.

"Thank you for taking care of my mother," she said. "The medicine you bring always makes her feel better."

"Yes, and there is something else that can help too," the Kamua had said. "Sharing the light – our own sense of inner joy and strength – can add to the healing."

The light, Miri had thought, remembering how, years earlier, Makena had also talked about the light.

Going back inside, Miri saw her that her mother was resting, her eyes closed. Watching the slow, even breaths, Miri imagined she saw a faint glow surrounding her, almost like she was sleeping in a warm blanket of love. She had a faint smile on her face. She looked content. Miri was thankful for what the Kamua had done. Even though her mother was very sick, she had brought happiness to her, if only for a little while. Miri sat and thought about that for a long time.

Soon after, her mother had passed on in what the people of Alumanaya considered the next step of life.

Miri spent a great deal of time walking along the beach thinking about her life and how things didn't feel the same anymore. Her happy island world had changed. She often couldn't sleep and late one night she took a walk to Lookout Rock. Climbing all the way out to the end, she looked up at the stars cascading across the sky. She found her favorite, Orana.

Will I ever be happy again? she thought, as the tears came once again. "What should I do?" she asked the tiny flickering pinpoints of light.

Her mother's words came back to her so clearly it felt like she could hear her voice, "There are many ways to bring joy into the world. Someday you will find what's right for you."

At that moment, Miri did know. She would become a Kamua like the one who had cared for her mother in her last days. That would be her way of bringing joy into the world.

Miri had then gone back to Makena for additional teaching. After much time learning and working with the other healers in the village, Miri was ready for her own patients. She was anxious to get started.

She had quickly settled in to her new life as a Kamua. After time, the sadness of her mother's passing faded and her natural state of happiness and joy returned. She loved working with her patients and, even though there were many difficult days, she was grateful for the opportunity to help bring light to so many lives. She didn't realize the next twist her life was about to take.

One day, just as she was leaving for her visits, the leader of the village came to her house. He talked about how the people on the other side of the island needed another healer to help with the growing community there. He said the elders had decided that Miri, with her exceptional skills, would be the best one to go to the windward village.

"It is your decision, but I hope you will consider how much you are needed by your fellow islanders," he had said.

For several days, Miri struggled with what to do. She had many questions and doubts. What if she didn't like living in the windward village? Were things different there? Who would take care of her patients? She was comfortable in her life here. This new change felt scary. But then she thought of the words of the leader, how he had talked about how much she could help. She imagined people on the other side of the island trying to live without the care they needed. Finally, the answer became clear. She would go to the other village.

"How long will it take to get there?" Rumbi's voice brought Miri back to the present.

"It won't take that long, especially if we do things a certain way," she replied.

"What do you mean do things a certain way?" he asked.

"Well, our goal is to get to your village, right? I know you are anxious to get home and, like we talked about earlier, it helps to think of all the reasons why. That keeps you interested in reaching your goal. But we also should remember to have fun along the way," Miri said.

"Fun is happy," said Rumbi, nodding.

Miri laughed, sometimes Rumbi said things just perfectly. "Yes, fun is happy. And there are so many ways to have fun and make our journey enjoyable. We need to pay attention as we go. If we only focus on looking to our goal far ahead, we'll miss a lot of nice things along the way.

"Let's play a game. As we walk, lets see how many different colors we see."

"OK," said Rumbi, spinning around. "I see yellow flowers and orange flowers and red flowers."

"I see the blue sky," said Miri.

"I see white clouds in the blue sky," said Rumbi.

"I see a green bird flying in the blue sky with white clouds," said Miri.

"The green bird has a brown beak," said Rumbi.

They were both shouting out colors now, "A purple vine . . . red lava rocks . . . black dirt . . . silver spider web . . . tan bark . . . gray air . . ."

"Wait a minute," said Miri. "Gray air?"

"Yes," Rumbi said. "Up there." He pointed to the big mountain far in the distance. The clouds covering the top did look a little like gray air.

"Yes, I see what you mean. That's where we're going. The trail takes us high up on the volcano. We'll be up in those clouds," Miri said.

"We're walking all the way up there?" asked Rumbi, his eyes wide.

"Yes. As I said before, this is a long journey. But we'll get up there before you know it. Look how far we've already come," she pointed back down the trail. They could barely see the village, far behind them.

"And we walked a long way while we were looking at colors. I think we saw every color on our island."

"We forgot one color," Rumbi said. "Polo."

"Polo?" Miri said, looking at the parrot sitting on Rumbi's shoulder. Polo's feathers were a rainbow of blues, greens, yellows, oranges and reds.

"Yes, Polo," Rumbi said. "That's where something is many colors. That's why I named him Polo."

"Hmmmm," Miri said, working through Rumbi's little-boy logic. "So, Polo was a sort of multi-color first and your parrot just happened to be that color."

"That's right. There are a lot of things colored polo, haven't you ever seen them?" Rumbi said.

"Well . . . "

"Look over there," Rumbi said, pointing at a thick tangle of vines containing many different colored flowers. "What color are all those?"

"Polo?" Miri asked.

"Polo," Rumbi confirmed.

"Yes, I guess you're right," Miri said. "I just never thought of it that way before." Once again, Miri was struck by how simple yet profound a child's understanding of the world could be. *Sometimes that may be the best way to look at things*, she decided.

They continued walking, gradually heading up into the hills. As they went, they both pointed out the beautiful and interesting things they saw. They appreciated the sweet scent of the flowers and the strange shapes of the lava rocks. They laughed at the funny shadows created by the sunlight shining through the swaying palm trees. At one point they sang, their footsteps beating out a rhythm on the reddish-brown dirt of the trail. All the while, moving steadily towards the mountain.

🌴 🌴 🌴 🌴 🌴 🌴 🌴

It was late in the day when Miri said, "Lets start looking for a good place to stop for the night." They had come a long way today and she knew Rumbi was getting tired. She was tired too.

"Do you hear that?" Rumbi said, turning his head to listen to what sounded like a low roar.

"It sounds like water," said Miri.

As they walked a little further, the sound grew louder until the trees opened up to reveal a waterfall splashing into a small pond.

"This looks like a good place to stop. What do you think?" Miri asked.

"Yes, this is great!" said Rumbi. He ran over to the edge of the water and kneeled down to look. "I see a fish in there. Should I catch him to cook for dinner?" He was hoping that Miri remembered he was a brave fisherman.

"Well, maybe he can just keep us company while we stay here," Miri said as she laid down her bag. She saw banana and mango trees growing around the pond. They would have enough to eat here without taking the time to prepare the fish. She wanted to settle down early and make sure they both got plenty of rest. Tomorrow they would need a lot of energy to get up the mountain.

"First, we need to make a place to sleep," Miri said.

They collected palm fronds that had fallen from the trees and stacked them several layers deep. Over the top, Miri laid one of the blankets she had brought. There was no covering overhead, but it didn't look like it would rain.

"This will work just fine," she said to Rumbi. "Now, lets go find our dinner."

They picked fruit from the trees around the pond and sat down to eat and talk about the day. They each picked out their favorite things they had seen and laughed about the silly songs they had made up. As the light faded away, they listened to the night bugs start their own songs.

"All right, it's time for all travelers to get some sleep," Miri said as she lay down on the palm bed.

Rumbi snuggled up next to her.

"Have sweet dreams," Miri said.

"I can't wait to see more fun things tomorrow," Rumbi said as he closed his eyes. He was asleep almost immediately.

Miri lay awake much longer. The trip had gone well so far, but she knew tomorrow would bring the first real challenge. They would be going high up the mountain. The trail would get much steeper, but she knew they could handle that part. She was worried about the volcano. It hadn't erupted in many years, since before she was born. But she knew that could change at any time. One time, when she was a little girl, the volcano had started to belch smoke and rumble. The people of the village all said that soon it would spit out fire and liquid rock. Miri had been scared. But after a few days, the smoke blew away and the volcano quieted down.

"Someday, Kapa Ohono will speak much louder," she had heard one of the older villagers say.

Tomorrow they would be very close to the mouth of the volcano. She hoped Kapa Ohono would remain quiet as they passed.

The next morning, Miri and Rumbi had a quick breakfast and set out. Soon, the trail became much steeper, winding back and forth across the hills as it led up the side of the mountain. After they had walked for a while, they came to a small clearing in the trees.

"Look at how high we are," Miri said, turning to look out towards the ocean.

The jungle-like canopy of green below gave way to a vast sea of blue that stretched as far as they could see. Way out on the horizon the blue abruptly switched shades where the water met the sky.

"I feel like a bird," Rumbi said. "Polo, is this what things look like when you fly?"

Polo didn't answer. He was eyeing another macadamia nut tree.

"The village is way down there," Miri said, pointing to a spot far off in the blanket of green.

They couldn't see any of the houses or even the open area where the celebration had been. Rumbi could just barely see a thin ribbon of white sand where they had watched the sea turtles crawl ashore to lay their eggs.

"We've come quite a distance, but we still have a long way to go. The trail will get even steeper now," Miri said. "We'd better get moving. We want to get close to the top before it gets dark."

Rumbi turned and looked up at the thick clouds surrounding the upper mountain. They were much closer to them now.

"We're going up there?" he asked, still unsure about getting so close to the volcano.

"Yes, we'll walk through those clouds. We may even find ourselves above them," Miri said.

Walk above the clouds? Rumbi thought. *How could we do that?*

They continued up the trail, stopping often to rest. They passed numerous streams and waterfalls running down from the mountain. The trail seemed to be damp and Rumbi noticed that there were little beads of water glistening on the plants and palm leaves.

"Up this high, it rains often," Miri explained. "That's why we've seen so many waterfalls."

Up ahead, the trail seemed to disappear into the haze.

"We're starting to get into the clouds now," Miri said.

"But how will we know which way to go?" Rumbi asked.

"We'll just make sure we stay on the trail," Miri replied. "Even though we can't see very far ahead, we have to trust that we are on the right path and it's taking us in the direction we are supposed to go. All we have to do is concentrate on each step we take, one after the other, with the proper ground beneath our feet. That way, we'll make it through the clouds."

They continued on, Rumbi following Miri through the mist. The thick air seemed to be closing in around them, shutting out the rest of the world. There were no sounds but their soft footsteps on the spongy trail. They could only see a few feet on either side before the trees faded into the murky gray air. Rumbi was beginning to have doubts.

"Maybe we should turn around," he said.

"I thought you wanted to go home?" Miri said. "Don't you want to see your Nanua and your aunt and the waves again?"

"Yes, but . . . it's getting dark and . . . "

"I know it's hard and a little scary," Miri said. "But we often have to go through something difficult in order to get to where we want to go. Remember how your Nanua taught you about the light, how it's always there even when we can't actually see it?"

"Yes," Rumbi said.

"Well, she's right. The light is always there. Right now it's shining up above our heads even though we can't see it because of the clouds. Imagine the light, Rumbi. Feel the light shining through the clouds and soaking into your skin, filling up your whole body with energy, strength and courage."

Rumbi tried to do as Miri said. After a moment, he smiled. "It kind of feels like I'm glowing inside. It feels warm."

"Good!" Miri said. "You are feeling the light. See how that helps?"

"I just thought of something else," Rumbi said. "When I'm watching the sunset with Nanua, I always like how the light bounces off the waves when the sun is sinking into the ocean. Sometimes it looks like a path on the water."

"Yes, that's a good thought," Miri said. "Maybe you should think of that now and imagine you are following the sunlight on the water. It's leading you back to your village. You are following the light home."

"Let's keep going," Rumbi decided. "These clouds aren't so bad and I do want to get home. Nanua probably misses watching the sunset with me."

162

"I'm sure she does," Miri said. "And we'll be home soon, but we still have a ways to go."

As they continued up the trail, Miri found she was feeling a little fearful too. She had only been on this trail once before. She hoped they were still going the right way. *There is just one trail across the island, isn't there?* she wondered. She decided to take her own advice and think about the light too. She thought of Rumbi's vision of the light on the ocean and smiled as she thought how that was something that could help him in many difficult situations. She had her own favorite way to think of the light – one she had learned long ago when she had made this journey across the island for the first time. She remembered that now and found that it brought her the same comfort it always did. She also thought of the other things Makena has taught her long ago. Soon she would be seeing Makena again, along with others in the village. It seemed like she had been gone a long time. Miri realized she was looking forward to going home too.

It was growing dark when Miri decided it was time to stop for the night. Up this high, there were fewer trees and plants. The ground was mostly old lava that had spewed from the volcano long ago. The clouds were thick now, and it was cooling off rapidly.

Miri found a spot just off the trail next to a large rock and dropped her bag. "This is a good place to stay tonight," she said. "The first thing we need to do is build a fire. It's starting to get cold, isn't it?"

"Yes," said Rumbi, shivering a little, "and I'm hungry."

"Here, this will help," said Miri, pulling a blanket from her bag. "We've got some good things to eat in here too."

Nearby they found some fallen palm branches and pieces of an old tree. Miri quickly had a warm fire going, the flickering flames causing shadows to dance on the big rock. They ate some of the fruit and nuts Miri had brought and talked about their hike up the mountain.

"How much further do we have to go?" Rumbi asked.

"Well, we're about halfway I think," said Miri. "Tomorrow we'll be heading back down the other side of the mountain. It will be a little easier since we'll be going downhill, but it will still take another couple of days to get to the village."

"Are we close to the mouth of Kapa Ohono?" Rumbi asked. He was thinking about the many stories he had heard about the volcano. He had always thought of it as some sort of living thing that sometimes got angry and spit out fire and hot rock. To Rumbi, it felt like they were sitting right on the shoulder of a sleeping monster. He hoped it wouldn't notice them.

"Yes, but we won't be going much higher. I think the trail soon starts to head back down," Miri answered. "Don't worry, Rumbi, the volcano hasn't erupted for a very long time. I don't think Kapa Ohono will mind if we stay here tonight."

They wrapped themselves in the blanket and huddled together against the rock. Even with the fire crackling in front of them, it was cold.

"Watch this," said Miri. She took a deep breath and slowly exhaled.

Rumbi was amazed. Miri was blowing smoke out of her mouth!

Miri laughed at Rumbi's wide-eyed look.

"Do you want to try?" she asked. "Take a deep breath and slowly blow it out."

Rumbi did and saw his breath turn to smoke the same way Miri's had.

Miri explained, "When it's this cold, you can see your breath. I guess we're like little volcanoes too!"

"Watch this one," Rumbi said, blowing out an even bigger breath.

Miri did it again too. They both laughed and puffed until they wore themselves out.

Finally, Miri said, "OK, that's enough. If we keep this up, there will be so much smoke we'll never be able to see the trail. It's time to get some sleep. We've got another big day tomorrow."

Rumbi snuggled in closer to her and was soon asleep. As Miri gazed at the fire she noticed how the clouds seemed to be thicker. It was almost like they did add their own smoke to the air. She thought she smelled something different in the dense haze, a slight odor that was hot and foul, like it came from deep in the earth. *It's just the fire*, she told herself as she closed her eyes.

As she drifted off to sleep, she dreamed that she and Rumbi were in a canoe roaring down the side of a huge wave. But the water was different. Instead of the deep blue of the ocean, it was bright orange and very hot. In her dream, she didn't hear the deep rumble that echoed down from the top of the volcano.

"SQUAAACK!" Polo blasted, jolting Miri awake. "SQUAAACK!" he cried again.

Miri opened her eyes to see the agitated parrot hopping and bobbing on the small rock where he had perched.

Why is he so upset? she wondered. Looking around, she saw how the haze was very thick now. In fact, instead of mist it looked like . . . it was smoke! And the foul smell was now very strong. Then she felt the ground tremble. The logs of the fire shifted, sending sparks high into the air.

It couldn't be! she thought, her mind refusing to grasp what seemed to be happening.

"Rumbi, wake up!" she said, shaking his shoulder.

What should we do? Should we run down the trail? Which way? Was this really happening?

"Is it morning?" asked Rumbi, rubbing his eyes. "It's still dark . . . what is that . . . "

Rumbi's question was cut short by an enormous blast from the top of the volcano. Fire shot high in the sky, cutting through the smoke and lighting up the night. The volcano was erupting!

"RUN!" shouted Miri, jumping up and grabbing Rumbi's hand. The smoke was so thick they could barely see or breathe. Gusts of hot air flowing down from above were pushing them down the mountain. They stumbled across rocks and brush as flecks of ash began to fall all around them. Another explosion rocked the hills, knocking them down.

"We've got to keep moving!" Miri said as she got up and pulled Rumbi back to his feet. They were headed down, but Miri didn't know which way they were going. Behind them she could see a bright orange glow. It was getting closer.

Liquid rock! she thought in a panic.

"KEEP GOING!" she shouted to Rumbi. They were running as fast as they could, but the trees were getting thicker as they moved downward and waves of smoke made it hard to see what was ahead. Miri knew they had to get as far away as possible. She remembered the stories of how the liquid rock would flow down the sides of the volcano, destroying everything in its path. But didn't it move slowly? Maybe they could outrun it.

Another blast of heat and ash rolled down the mountain, pushing them forward. Suddenly the ground gave way beneath them and they were falling! They tumbled and rolled down a steep hill for what seemed like forever.

Finally, they came to a stop. Miri was groggy from the fall.

"Rumbi, are you hurt?" she asked.

"I . . . I don't think so," he said, slowly getting up.

They were in a ravine that had been carved by water running down the hills during countless rainstorms. Even though they had plunged far down the mountain, Miri knew they were still in great danger. If water could flow down the ravine, the liquid rock could too. She knew it wouldn't be long before it would come, consuming everything in its path.

"Come on, we've got to get to higher ground," she said as she got unsteadily to her feet.

They climbed up the side of a large rock. Miri struggled over the edge to the flat top and reached back to pull Rumbi up. Sitting down, she found she was breathing hard and was dizzy. She didn't feel well at all.

"Let's rest here for a minute, then we'll . . ." Suddenly, Miri slumped over.

"Miri! What's wrong?" Rumbi cried. "Miri, wake up!" He shook her shoulders and patted her cheeks. What had happened to Miri? She was still breathing, but her eyes were closed. It looked like she had suddenly fallen asleep.

What should I do? he thought. *Miri is hurt and the liquid rock is coming after us!* Rumbi was scared.

"HELP!" he cried as loudly as he could. "HELP. . . NANUA . . . " His only answer was another deep rumble from the volcano.

In Makena's dream she was in a roaring storm. Thunder rocked the air and the ground beneath her while lightning streaked across the sky. She was searching for her grandson but the sheets of rain made it hard to see.

"RUUUMMMBIIII!" she called, "RUMBI, WHERE ARE YOU?"

She was startled awake and sat up in her bed. *What was that?* She thought she had heard someone answering her, calling her name – a faint, small voice . . . Rumbi? Then she heard a deep rumble. Was that the thunder she had been dreaming about? No, it was different, much deeper. Like it was coming from the ground itself.

She looked over at her sister, Anate, who was asleep in a hammock. Anate had been staying with Makena since Rumbi had disappeared. He had been missing now for several days. Practically the whole village had been looking for him, scouring the nearby jungle and beaches for any sign of the boy. Just before nightfall it was discovered that one of the small canoes was missing. Had he gone out in the ocean? A few nights ago a tremendous storm had passed over the island. If Rumbi had been caught out on the water in that storm . . . Makena refused to think about that. Maybe he had followed a bird or a monkey into the jungle and was lost. Rumbi loved to explore and learn new things about the island, but he had never before gone too far from the village. He had always returned in time to sit with her and watch the sunset. Where was he?

Lying down again, she listened to the night sounds. No, there was nothing unusual to be heard. No voice calling for help. She had thought she had heard it so clearly, but it must have been a dream. Through her window, she could see the glittering stars in the cloudless sky. There was no storm. Maybe she had dreamed the thunder-like sound too. She closed her eyes and thought of her grandson. She pictured walking with him along the beach listening to the ocean waves and softly said, "Wherever you are, Rumbi, it is alright. Remember what I taught you. You'll be home again soon." The soothing thoughts calmed her. She was sleeping again as the thick smoke and ash slowly crept across the sky over the village. One by one, the stars blinked out.

Rumbi was terrified. The ground continued to rumble, and high up on the mountain, the orange glow was getting brighter. The falling ash was turning everything white and hot winds were sweeping down the hills.

What can I do? he thought. *Miri is hurt, so we can't run . . . The liquid rock is coming . . . Kapa Ohono is trying to eat us . . . I'll never see my Nanua or my aunt or Polo or my home again!*

Rumbi sat next to Miri and hugged his knees to his chest. Feeling very small, alone and afraid, he closed his eyes tight. He thought of his home – the beach, the palm trees, the ocean water. He longed for the safe feeling of everything familiar. He began to cry as he thought of how his Nanua and his aunt must miss him, wondering where he was. *I'm not a brave fisherman, why did I ever get in that canoe?* It seemed so long ago that he and Polo had paddled out into the ocean, just looking to catch a fish. The bright clear day had turned into the angry, stormy night. He remembered how scared he had been then, with the little canoe tossing around on the big waves.

Thinking of the storm at sea, he remembered how the words of Makena had helped him to feel better. Would they help again now? He had made it through the punamu, could he could make it through this too? Rumbi thought that, even if he wasn't brave, maybe he could at least act brave. He decided to try.

Just then, he thought he heard a voice, "Wherever you are, Rumbi, it is alright. Remember what I taught you. You'll be home again soon." His eyes flew open. "Nanua? Are you here?" he said. All he could see was falling ash and billowing smoke. *She's not really here*, he thought. *But I'm going to do what she taught me.*

Breathe in only what you need, Rumbi thought, remembering Makena's teachings of the wind. He closed his eyes and took a deep breath and coughed from the thick air. He realized the first thing he needed to do was make some sort of mask to filter the ash and smoke. Looking around, he found a sharp rock and cut a strip of cloth from the bottom of Miri's long skirt. He wrapped it around his head, covering his mouth. This helped a lot. *Let the winds of trouble sweep past you*, he remembered. Right now, the winds really *were* blowing, so it was easy to visualize them flowing past. He cut another strip and covered Miri's mouth too. He saw that her breathing was still slow and steady. Rumbi hoped that was a good sign, but the falling ash was covering everything, turning Miri's dark hair white.

We've got to get under some cover, he thought, *or the ash will bury us*.

Nearby, there were several palm trees that had grown to meet at the top, forming an arch. Rumbi had an idea. He bent over and put his arms around Miri's waist and tried to pick her up. She didn't budge. Thinking for a moment, he moved around behind her and put his hands under her shoulders. Pulling as hard as he could, he tried to drag her towards the trees. She moved a few inches. He pulled again, she moved a little more. It was still a long way to the trees, could he pull Miri that far? Then he remembered something else Makena had taught. The light. He imagined being filled with a bright white glow. It was flowing through his body and giving him strength. He pulled again, moving Miri a little closer. It was working! Rumbi knew that even though it would take a while, he was going to do it.

He pulled and pulled until finally, Miri was under the trees. He then gathered some palm fronds and leaned them against the curved trunks. He crawled into the shelter with Miri to think of what to do next.

"Our real goal is not so much to get to the destination, but to be happy along the way."

- Miri

Makena opened her eyes. It was still dark and she could hear shouting.

What is going on? she wondered. *What is all this excitement in the middle of the night?*

Still half asleep, she rose from her bed and went to the door. Looking out towards the village, she could see a number of torches moving around. People were clustered in the gathering area. Out on the horizon, there was a dull orange glow where the sun normally rose. The sky above was still dark, but in a strange sort of way. There seemed to be a kind of haze in the air. Taking a few steps outside, she felt something falling on the skin of her arms. It felt a little like a light mist, only dry. And, rather than the sweet scent of jasmine that would normally greet her, she smelled a sharp odor like . . . like . . . Suddenly she knew was happening. The volcano! She realized what she was feeling on her skin was ash falling from an eruption. It was smoke that was blanketing the sky, obscuring the dawn and filling the air with a pungent sulfur smell.

She woke Anate and they quickly made their way down the hill to the other villagers. Nearing the crowd, they could hear the frantic talk. The islanders were trying to decide what to do.

"We must get everyone out of the village. Move to the high rocks down the beach," one person said.

"Gather all the goats and chickens too," another added.

"We should first create a barrier to stop the liquid rock, so we can save our houses," someone else said.

"No, no, nothing can stop the liquid rock. We must all get in canoes and paddle out into the ocean," another cried.

"Quiet! Everyone calm down!" They all turned as the village chief joined the group.

"It appears that Kapa Ohono has broken his long silence," he said. "While we have all hoped for many more years of quiet, we must realize that the volcano is as much a part of our island as we are. Remember, long, long ago Kapa Ohono rose from the ocean, breathing fire and growing into this island we call home. And, many generations from now, he will continue to speak to the people of Alumanaya. This is natural. What we need to do now is understand what he is saying. We need to find out what changes the eruption has already caused and what more may come."

By now everyone in the village was together in the gathering area. The crowd was quiet as the chief spoke.

The oldest member of their community, he was one of the few remaining people who had experienced the last major eruption many years ago. At that time, the liquid rock had flowed right through the village as it made its way to the ocean. Although no one had perished, virtually every house and building had been destroyed. The elders had realized that they needed to find a better location to rebuild and had moved several miles up the beach to the site of the present village. Not only did the new location have an excellent harbor for fishing, but more importantly, the hills above provided protection from future eruptions. The hot, liquid rock would be diverted through the gullies away from the houses. As a boy helping to restore the village, the future chief knew the islanders would be safe for generations to come. He reminded the others of this now.

"Remember the foresight of those before us," he said. "The liquid rock will not come our way. Our houses are safe. But we must learn what damage has been done and if Kapa Ohono is finished for now. Most importantly, we must come to the aid of our fellow Alumanayans. The village on the other side is much closer to the volcano. We must travel up the trail and to the other side to see what has happened and to help in any way we can."

The crowd began to murmur again. Calmed of their immediate fears by the chief's words, their concern now turned to the people on the other side of the island.

"Let's go immediately," one person said.

"I'll bring tools to rebuild," another said.

Soon, a number of villagers had volunteered to make the journey. Others began to plan what food and supplies would be needed. The chief, being too old to travel very far, appointed a strong young man to lead the group.

As Makena watched, she felt the desire to go along too. She knew she could help with any injuries they may find in the other village as well as care for any of the rescuers along the way. But there was something more. She felt something else was calling her to make this journey. What was this other feeling she had?

"I'm going too," she said, stepping over to the rescue party leader. "I'll gather medicines and bandages to take along."

The group quieted. Makena was one of the most respected people in the village. She had taught most of the younger islanders the ways of the island and was the one many of them still came to in times of difficulty. They were hesitant for her to go.

The young leader paused and looked into Makena's eyes. In them, he saw the strength that he had learned from her when he was a boy, which to him, suddenly seemed not so long ago. He stepped forward and hugged her. "Thank you," he whispered in her ear. He knew her presence would bring courage and wisdom not only to him, but to all of the rescuers and to any situation they may encounter on their journey.

Turning to Anate, Makena said, "You should stay here in case Rumbi is found."

Her sister nodded and hugged Makena. "Remember the light," she said.

"Well then," Makena said to the rescue leader. "Let's get busy. We have a lot to do before we leave."

"Breathe in only what you need. Let the
rest flow on past."
- Makena

It was morning.

Rumbi sat under the shelter and watched the ash fall. In the hazy light, it looked like they were on a new island. The jungle had changed. Instead of shades of green splashed with bright colors, it was now a uniform white. The ash covered everything.

This must be what it looks like on the moon, he thought.

Miri lay beside him. She was breathing deeply but still had not opened her eyes. Rumbi had hoped that she would be awake by now. She would know what to do. At least the volcano had quieted down. There had not been any more rumblings for a while.

Should I try to go get help? he wondered. *But which way would I go? Where is the trail? I don't even know how far it is to either village!*

"Polo, maybe you should go get help," he said. "Polo . . . Polo?" He jumped up and looked all around. The parrot was nowhere to be seen.

"POLO, WHERE ARE YOU?" he called.

He listened hard for a familiar *squaaack* but heard nothing, not even the common chirps and rustlings of a new morning. Rumbi felt very alone in this strange white world.

Again, he remembered the words of Makena. Closing his eyes, he took a deep breath. *I'm taking in only what I need*, he thought. *The rest of the trouble winds are blowing past.*

"You are breathing in only what you need too," he said, sitting down next down next to Miri.

He took Miri's hand in his like he had seen her do with her patients. "I'm going to take care of you now," he said. "Things will be OK. The light is helping you and showing me what to do."

Rumbi felt his courage rising – like some kind of power was slowly filling him up inside. Miri shifted and mumbled, but didn't wake up.

"Yes, things will be OK," he confirmed again. "I will take care of us both."

"I'm going to find some water and something for us to eat," he said to Miri, picking up her bag. "I'll be back soon. If you wake up while I'm gone, call my name. I won't be far away."

Rumbi crawled out of the shelter into the white ash. It wasn't falling quite as heavily now, but the air was still thick and hard to breath. He wrapped the cloth across his mouth and set off to see what he could find.

He kicked at the soft ash as he walked. As it flew into the air, it reminded Rumbi of the white sand on the beach. He remembered Makena teaching him how the sand was like thoughts, always being moved around by the winds and water, but always ultimately under our own control. He decided to think of the ash as just more sand, which made him feel better.

"The beach has moved up to the mountain," he said aloud and smiled as he pictured grains of sand running up the hills on little legs.

He heard something that sounded familiar. *Maybe the ocean came too*, he thought as he realized it sounded like water.

He followed the sound down the hill to find a small creek tumbling swiftly over the rocks. He found the water pouch in Miri's bag and knelt down. The fast moving stream looked clear of any ash so he plunged the pouch deep into the water. It quickly filled.

"OK, now lets find something to eat," he said. He was pretending to talk with Polo. It made him feel a little less alone. He hoped Polo was OK, wherever he was.

Rumbi followed his tracks in the ash back up the hill. As he got close to the shelter, he noticed a big mango tree. Covered in a blanket of white, he had not recognized it before.

He picked several of the ripe fruit and ducked back into the shelter.

"I found food and water," he said to Miri. "Let's have breakfast."

He raised Miri's head with one hand and held the water pouch to her lips. He squeezed a little into her mouth. It looked like she was swallowing it.

"Good! Now lets eat," he said.

He peeled the skin from a mango. *How can she eat this?* he wondered.

Thinking for a moment, he remembered the small parrot the old woodcarver had given him. He found it in his bag along with something else – his lucky rock. He tore off a piece of the fruit, put it on the rock and used the wooden parrot to mash it into a pulp.

Lifting Miri's head again, he put a little bit into her mouth. She swallowed it like she had the water.

"That's the way!" Rumbi said. "You'll be strong again soon!"

He continued to eat and feed Miri until the fruit was gone.

"Now, lets take a nap. It's been a long night," he said, lying down next to her. "Later, I'll get more for us to eat."

Rumbi was soon asleep. He dreamed he was out in his canoe again, but this time there was no storm. The sky was bright blue and the sun sparkled on the water. There was something flipping and flopping in his fishing net as he tried to pull it in. It was the biggest fish he had ever seen! He couldn't wait to show his Nanua. He was a brave fisherman after all.

Makena and the rest of the rescue party made their way up the mountain, following the trail leading to the other side. As she walked, Makena thought about Rumbi. Not only had the storm a few nights ago made the ocean dangerous, but now the eruption of the volcano had rocked the island as well. Wherever he might be, these events had made things much harder for him.

While she was gone, she knew that others in the village would continue to look for her grandson. But even as they continued the search, Makena knew that some were starting to think he might never be found. They wondered how such a little boy could survive on his own for so long. But Makena thought differently. She continued to think that Rumbi would be coming home. She had seen the light in him and knew he would remember all she had taught. Maybe he would be there by the time she returned from this journey. In her mind, she pictured him hopping and dancing on the beach, running into her arms to welcome her back. As she continued up through the ash, she concentrated on remembering the sound of Rumbi's laughter as he played in the waves.

When Rumbi awoke later in the day, the ash from the volcano had stopped falling. While the sky was still hazy with smoke, it was a little brighter.

Miri hadn't moved. Watching her sleep, Rumbi tried to think of something else he could do. Deciding more food and water might help, he left the shelter and made his way down to the creek again. While he was filling the water pouch, he saw something move in the brush a few feet away. It was a gecko! It scurried to the top of a rock and stood staring at Rumbi, a bright green splash against the white ash background.

"Hey there, have you seen a lost parrot anywhere?" Rumbi asked.

The gecko blinked and Rumbi laughed. "OK, well if you do, tell him I'm right up there in those trees," he said pointing up the hill. Seeing the gecko brightened his spirits. It reminded him of home and of ordinary things.

On his way back to the shelter, he picked more fruit from the mango tree. Looking around, he thought he spotted a coconut tree a little further up the hill.

That sounds good. Miri likes coconuts, he thought as he climbed up the hill.

Standing at the base of the tree, he looked at the cluster hanging high above. In the past, he had watched the older boys of the village climb the tall trees to retrieve the fruit. It had looked easy. Just scamper up the curved trunk and back down again. Rumbi was sure he could do it too. He put down the bag and started up.

The climb was easy at first, but as the trunk straightened out, it became much harder. Rumbi wrapped his arms around the trunk and inched his way up. The coconuts were still a few feet above when he looked down for the first time. He was startled. The tree didn't look this tall from the ground!

Should I keep going? he wondered, a little fear creeping in.

He tried to move a little higher, but his foot slipped. The ash had made the smooth bark even more slippery. Determined to reach his goal, Rumbi dug into the trunk and reached higher. Suddenly, he lost his grip and was falling! He hit the ground with a thud.

Rumbi rolled over and sat up, shaking his head. It took a few seconds to realize what had happened. A sharp pain quickly reminded him. The ash had softened his fall, but he had landed on his arm and it hurt!

"OWWWW!" he wailed as tears filled his eyes. "MIRI . . . HELP!" he cried.

But Miri couldn't hear him. Rumbi quickly realized that. Nobody could hear him. He was stuck way up on the mountain, alone. Rumbi knew that he had to help himself. With this thought he started to feel something he didn't often experience. Anger.

"WHY DID THIS HAPPEN?" he yelled into the white silence. "Why did I ever go out in that stupid canoe? Why did the volcano have to erupt right when we were on our way home?" He stood up and kicked the coconut tree. "WHY DID YOU HAVE TO BE SO TALL?"

Rumbi stalked around in circles, kicking at the white ash. "This doesn't really look like sand! I want REAL sand and a REAL beach! I WANT TO GO HOME!" he yelled, his voice echoing through the hills.

Remembering his home made him think of Makena. And, as always, thinking of Makena made him remember the many things she had taught him. *Yes, the trouble winds are blowing, but they won't blow me over,* he thought with determination. *I'll be like the flexible palm tree, bending but not breaking.*

He slowly moved his sore arm around in circles. It still hurt but not nearly as much. "See," he said, looking up at the coconut tree. "You didn't hurt me. I'll be back later to get your coconuts. And I'll make sure to take every one!"

He turned and went back down the hill to the shelter. He didn't notice that he crossed over what looked like a trail – a trail that led down the mountain.

🌴🌴🌴🌴🌴🌴🌴

Rumbi spent the rest of the day in the shelter, feeding Miri and giving her water. He wet the cloth he had used earlier to cover his mouth and wiped the ash off of Miri's face. He combed the grit out of her hair with his fingers. All the while, he talked to her, telling her about seeing the gecko and climbing the coconut tree. He didn't know if she could hear him, but he thought it might make her feel better somehow. At least it helped him to feel better.

As it got dark, his talk switched to what they would do when they made it home. He told her about the village and his friends. How they often had celebrations just like the one in Miri's village a few nights earlier. He told her about his long talks with Makena and how she had recently taught him things to help in his life. How her words had helped him on this trip and would help him figure out how he could get them both home.

Finally, Rumbi was worn out from the long day.

"It's time to get some sleep," he said to Miri. "Tomorrow, I'll find more food. I may even get us some bananas! Don't worry Miri, we'll get home soon and Makena will be waiting for us."

He moved in close beside her and was soon asleep. He didn't feel Miri stir, or hear her softly mumble, "Makena."

※ ※ ※ ※ ※ ※ ※

Outside, the hot air rolling down from the mountain had shifted, giving way to the cooling trade winds that normally blew across the island. As the smoke gradually cleared, the stars started to appear. Orana slowly made it's way across the sky. A few night bugs tentatively called out. Soon, more of their friends answered. An owl sat blinking on a limb and added his voice to the chorus. The island was coming back to life.

"The journey starts now and lasts the rest of your life."

- Makena

It was just before sunrise when Makena and the rest of the rescue party left their overnight camp to continue up the mountain. Yesterday they had covered a great distance, especially after the ash had finally stopped falling. Today they hoped to get close to the top of the trail where it would then start to descend to the other village. As they walked, Makena and the rescue party leader looked for damage from the eruption. So far, all they had seen was the covering of ash, which got deeper the higher they went. There was no sign of the dangerous liquid rock flow. This was good for their village, but indicated that the flow may have run the other way, down towards the windward side where they were headed. Makena tried not to think about what they might find there.

As the sun rose and filtered through the palm trees it caused the grit in the ash to sparkle.

It looks a little like sand, Makena thought.

Makena shook her head as she thought about how quickly things can change. In a matter of hours, this green landscape had turned to white. A few days earlier, she had been walking on the beach with her grandson. Now he was gone. It seemed like she had been somehow dropped into another world. But she understood that eventually the island she knew would emerge from the blanket of ash. It was still there, only temporarily invisible. She hoped the same was true with Rumbi – that soon he would appear and once again sit with her to watch the sunset.

Lost in her thoughts, Makena had increased her pace to where she was far ahead of the rest of the group. A short chirp from the nearby brush snapped her back to the present. She smiled at the bright yellow bird hopping along a tree branch. It chirped again.

"Good morning, little friend," she said. "Are you trying to tell me something?"

She decided to stop and wait for the rest of the group to catch up. Looking ahead, up the trail, she noticed something odd. The ash looked different. Like something had shuffled around in a big circle, disturbing the smooth covering. Walking a little further, she saw what looked like tracks leading to the base of a tall coconut tree.

What sort of animal could have done this? she wondered.

Then, she saw more tracks leading the other way, down the hill. These were much clearer. They looked like footprints. Small ones.

Makena waved at the approaching group, "Hurry, I think I've found something."

She quickly crossed the trail and ran down the hill, following the tracks. They lead her around a big rock to a grove of small palm trees. It looked like someone had stacked up palm fronds, creating a shelter.

"Hello, is there anyone in there?" she called, moving closer to look inside.

In the dim light, she saw a woman lying on her back. Was she alive? Then, something next to the woman moved. It was another, smaller, person. It was . . . RUMBI!

For a moment, Makena was stunned. For days she had been thinking of Rumbi, picturing his face in her mind. Was he really here? Or had her hopes gone too far and created an illusion that would be gone with the next blink of an eye?

But all her fears vanished when Rumbi opened his eyes. "NANUA!" he shouted, jumping up into her arms.

Rumbi hugged Makena as hard as he could and started to babble, "I went out in my canoe to catch a fish and a big storm came up and then a sea turtle pushed me to another beach and Miri found me and then the volcano erupted and she got hurt and I fell out of the coconut tree and . . . " he paused to catch a breath.

"Slow down, slow down," said Makena as she wiped tears from her eyes. "You can tell me all about your adventure soon. But first, are you all right? And, did you say . . . Miri?"

"Yes, I'm OK," Rumbi said, rubbing his arm. It still hurt a little but he decided not to say anything about it. "Miri got hurt when we fell down the mountain. I've been taking care of her. She said you taught her too."

"Yes, I did," Makena said. It had been many years since she had seen Miri. Makena remembered when her young student had decided she wanted to be a healer. How hard Miri had worked to learn the techniques of helping others. Makena had been very proud when, in a solemn ceremony, Miri had been given the necklace of shells that signified she was a Kamua, one of the most revered groups of people on the island. Makena had always felt a special connection with Miri and had been sad when Miri left to go to the windward village. She hadn't expected to see her again, especially not in the gloom of a makeshift shelter high on the mountain.

Makena bent to look closer. She couldn't see any obvious injuries except for a small bruise on her forehead. Miri appeared to be sleeping, the shell necklace rising and falling with each breath.

"Will she be all right?" Rumbi asked.

"I hope so," Makena answered. "We'll need to get her back down to the village right away where we can take better care of her."

Just then, the leader of the rescue group poked his head into the shelter.

"We need to get this one down to the village as soon as possible. She's hurt and needs more than I can do for her right here," Makena said. "And by the way, look who else I found."

Rumbi shyly stepped out of the shadows and was immediately wrapped up in the arms of the rescue leader. The rest of the group cheered. Their mission had already been a success! They had found their little lost friend!

It was quickly decided that two of the group would return to the village with Rumbi and Miri. Makena was torn as to what to do. She was concerned about what might be needed at the other village, but she also could see Miri needed care too. She was also hesitant to part with Rumbi again.

"Right now, you should be with your grandson," the rescue leader said to Makena. "And you need to take care of Miri. We can send for you later if we need to."

Makena reluctantly agreed and went to work building a stretcher to carry Miri. They were quickly ready to go and the groups parted. The rescue party headed on up the trail, while Makena and Rumbi led the way back down to the village.

As they walked, Rumbi told Makena about everything that had happened since he and Polo had climbed into the canoe. Makena was amazed at all that Rumbi had been through. She was especially impressed with how Rumbi had cared for Miri. She knew that he very well might have saved her life. *How could such a young boy have the strength to not only overcome his own fears, but help someone else too?* she wondered.

"When I got scared, I just remembered the things you had taught me," Rumbi said. "And it always seemed like everything turned out OK."

This was the best thing Makena could hear. She was overjoyed to think that Rumbi had not only heard her words but had applied them to his life when he needed them the most. She knew he would call upon those thoughts and ideas many times in the future and that they would help him for the rest of his life.

Even though the return trip down the mountain was a little easier than going up, the need to carry Miri meant the group couldn't move very fast. They still had a long way to go by the time it was getting dark. They found a place to stop for the night, built a fire, and laid out the food they had brought. As they ate, Rumbi helped Makena feed Miri, like he had done earlier. Throughout the day, Miri had periodically moved and mumbled. *That must be a good sign,* Rumbi thought. M*aybe she is coming out of her sleep.*

"We need to get some sleep too," Makena said. "Tomorrow, we'll try to make it home. We want to get an early start." They lay down on a bed of palm fronds. Rumbi was between Makena and Miri.

"I can't wait," said Rumbi. "I'm going straight to the ocean. I miss the waves."

"Yes, they've missed you too. And they will be happy to see another old friend," Makena said as she looked over at Miri.

Rumbi closed his eyes and reached for Makena's hand.

"Goodnight, Nanua," he said.

"Goodnight, Rumbi," Makena said. She smiled as she watched Rumbi take hold of Miri's hand too. As they lay beneath the stars, she felt something powerful – almost like a new beginning. She fell asleep and dreamed of the three of them holding hands again. This time while walking along the beach in the bright sunshine.

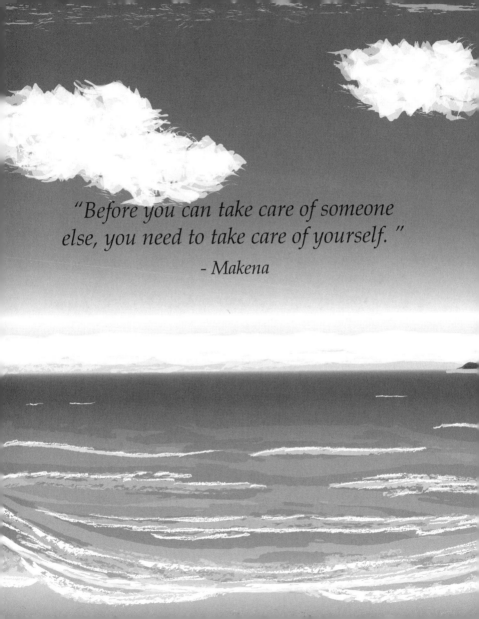

"*Before you can take care of someone else, you need to take care of yourself.*"

- Makena

"Rumbi, wake up," a soft voice said.

"Nanua?" Rumbi said sleepily. He opened his eyes to the early morning light. He looked over at his grandmother. She was still asleep. But then, who . . .

"Not Nanua, but close," the voice said.

Rolling over the other way, he looked into Miri's smiling eyes. She was awake!

"I knew you'd wake up!" Rumbi cried. "Nanua, wake up, Miri's fixed!"

"Fixed?" Miri laughed, "I didn't know I was broken! Owww, my head hurts. Stop making me laugh, it makes it worse!" But at the same time, she reached over to tickle Rumbi.

"What is going on here? Calm down you two," Makena said, sitting up.

Makena and Miri's eyes met. In an instant it felt like only yesterday they were parting ways, Miri heading off to her new life in the other village. They hugged as both sets of eyes filled with tears.

"Hey, you're squishing me," Rumbi cried, caught in the middle.

"Where are we? What happened?" Miri said as she and Makena separated. "The last thing I remember was the volcano erupting and we were running."

"We fell down the mountain," Rumbi said. "We bounced and rolled forever and when we finally stopped, you were asleep."

"You must have hit your head," Makena said. "Rumbi took care of you until we found you both." She told Miri how Rumbi had made the shelter and fed her water and fruit.

"You took care me?" she said, looking at Rumbi. "Thank you. You're my hero!"

Rumbi blushed and looked down. "I didn't do much. I . . . well, I found water . . . "

"We're on our way back to the leeward side," Makena said. "Another group is headed over to your village to see if there is any damage from the eruption."

"Oh no! I should go back . . . " Miri tried to stand but quickly sat back down. She was dizzy.

"The only place you are going is back to your home with me," Makena said firmly. "The others can take care of anyone on the other side. We've got to take care of you first."

"But . . . my patients . . . " Miri protested.

" . . . will be taken care of," Makena finished. "Remember what I taught you. Before you can heal someone else, you have to be healed yourself. You need a few days rest, then we'll see what to do next."

Makena knew how hard it was for Miri to accept not rushing back to help. But she also knew how important it was for Miri to recover first. She had seen many times how only caring for others instead of one's self had taken its toll. Then, both the healer and patient suffer.

Makena helped Miri stand up.

"Can you walk?" she asked.

"I think so," Miri said, taking a few steps. "But I'm not sure I can dance." She smiled as she looked at Rumbi. Rumbi smiled back. He loved Miri's sense of humor, even when he knew she didn't feel very good.

By now, the others were awake too. They put out the fire and were soon back on the trail headed down towards the village. Miri moved slowly at first, but after a while was feeling much better. As they walked, they talked about life on both sides of the island. Miri talked about her patients and the new friends she had made over the years. Makena filled her in on her old friends and family. They were making good time. They would be home by afternoon.

The sun was starting its daily fall into the ocean as the group made their way through the trees towards a clearing. Makena knew what lay just beyond and slowed to let Miri get a few steps ahead.

"We must be getting close, I . . . oh!" Miri said as she stepped into the sunshine. They were on a small bluff. Ahead, as far as she could see, was bright blue water. Below, nestled among the lush green trees, were the houses of the leeward village.

"I . . . I wondered if I would ever see this again," Miri said.

"Welcome home," Makena said, putting her arm around Miri. "Everyone will be happy to see you."

"Let's run!" said Rumbi, taking off down the trail. He knew the way from here and nothing was slowing him down now!

Rumbi ran all the way to the gathering area in the center of the village. He couldn't wait to see everything again; the fish in the stream, the familiar houses, even the old woman who always told him to quiet down! But first, he wanted to find his aunt. It didn't take long – she was the first one to see him.

"Rumbi!" Anate cried, rushing to pull him into her arms.

The other villagers quickly crowded around, excited that Rumbi was safely home. Rumbi soon felt like he was being squeezed to death by all the joyous hugs.

The rest of the group made its way into the village soon after. At first, the villagers didn't recognize the dark-haired woman walking alongside Makena. Then someone said, "It's Miri!"

Now it was Miri's turn. They flocked around her, some laughing, some crying, but all happy to see her too.

The crowd continued to grow. Rumbi and Miri were the center of attention as they took turns telling about the events over the past few days. They were all impressed with how Rumbi had made it through the storm and marveled at how he had climbed the coconut tree.

"It was 100 feet tall!" Rumbi said. He left out the part about falling. That didn't really matter anyway, he figured.

What impressed everyone the most was how Rumbi had taken care of Miri when she was hurt.

"Yes, he is my hero," Miri said, smiling at Rumbi who, ducking his head, blushed at the praise.

Suddenly there was a loud "SQUAAACK!" and, in a flurry of flapping color and dusty feathers, a very tired parrot landed on the grass at Rumbi's feet.

"Polo!" Rumbi shouted, picking up his friend.

Everyone cheered and laughed. The other missing villager was home too!

Rumbi sat down next to Makena with Polo perched on his shoulder. The talk turned to Miri's life the past few years. She told everyone how she had settled in the windward village and began her role as a Kamua. She talked about what went on day to day in her new home and answered the many questions everyone had in comparing life on both sides of the island.

As they sat, Makena felt Rumbi begin to squirm next to her. She looked down into his pleading brown eyes.

"OK, go ahead. I'll be there soon," she said. She knew just what Rumbi wanted to do. He was gone in a flash.

Makena continued to listen to Miri's talk about her life. Miri seemed very content in the path she had chosen. She brought a great deal of joy and happiness into her world every day and Makena knew that came from within Miri herself. She had learned to feel the light inside and then share her joy with others. That was truly the secret to helping.

Makena stood up and quietly made her way out of the crowd. Miri's voice faded as Makena went to join her grandson. She walked a short distance to where the palm trees opened up to a long, white beach. The warm sand under her feet connected her with the golden light of the setting sun. She closed her eyes and took a deep breath. The scent of jasmine filled the air. The trouble winds were gone. She said a quick prayer of thanks for her life, her island, for the sound of the ocean filling her ears, and finally, for the sweetest gift of all, the laughter of Rumbi as he played with his friends, the waves.

Alumanaya words and names

Anate (ah-NAH-tay)
Name of Rumbi's great aunt. Anate is Makena's sister.

Alumanaya (ah-loo-mah-NAY-ah)
Name of island. Also used to describe a calm, peaceful, joyous state of mind. A feeling of contentment, perspective and balance.

Ahani (ah-HAH-nee)
Gentle breeze. Can be used to describe a pleasant life experience.

Kahua (kah-HOO-ah)
Healer and/or teacher. The people of Alumanaya considered healing and teaching to be interdependent, one enhanced and was a part of the other. To become a Kahua, one would go through specific training emphasizing techniques of both physical and mental healthcare. A Kahua was greatly respected and held in high regard on the island.

Kikani (kee-KAH-nee)
Musical instrument. Resembles a guitar.

Makena (mah-KAY-nah)
Name of Rumbi's grandmother. The main Kahua on the island.

Melehono (may-lay-HO-no)
Name of the most popular musician on the island.

Miri (MIH-ree)
Name of the Kamua (healer) who finds Rumbi on the other side of the island.

Orana (o-RAH-nah)
Star constellation. Also known as Orion the Island Hunter.

Peule (pay-OOO-lay)
Name of the main village artist.

Polo (PO-lo)
Name of Rumbi's pet parrot.

Punamu (poo-NAH-moo)
Strong, hurricane-force wind. Also used to describe difficult life events. Sometimes referred to as "trouble wind."

Rumbi (RUM-bee)
Name of island boy who is learning the teachings of Alumanaya.

Thanks for reading!

If you would like to know more about Alumanaya or explore more of the island, there is always something new at:

www.alumanaya.com

Would your employees, co-workers or friends benefit from a feeling of Alumanaya?

Bulk book sales
Speaking events & Island Seminars
Island art for home or office

Contact:

Palm Canyon Wellness Group, LLC
P.O. Box 64
Cottleville, Missouri 63338
314-482-6152
info@alumanaya.com